Kiamichi Bill

"Kiamichi Bill" Burns traveled the Boomer Trail, fascinated with passing trains and railyard activity, but he had been content to remain a "blanket stiff." Then, one day he spoke aloud thoughts of the future — a steady job, a home …

His friend Blackie Burns, whose surname he had adopted, knew the score. "Listen, Kiamichi," Blackie interrupted. "You ain't foolin' me none. Jist one thing puts thoughts like that into a young feller's head — an' that one thing's a woman. I ain't object-in' nor criticizin'."

Blackie was correct — Bill was smitten with Lula Ross, the breath-taking redhead who considered him a hero. He joined the S. & S. when superintendant King Lawson offered him a job. Everything was falling into place, but the die was cast for trouble.

Conductor Charlie Ross held a hidden animosity toward Blackie, and transferred that anger to Bill. Along came "Duke" Wellington, a Brass Hat's nephew promoted well ahead of his experience and eager to make a play for Lula. Then Bill faced his greatest challenge — the deadly sidecar cabooses.

Also: "When the Devil Calls," a tale of the S. & S., and "Vengeance," a story of Rud Randall, engineer.

Other books in the Railroad Stories series

RAILROAD
STORIES

#6

"The Saga of Kiamichi Bill"

E.S. Dellinger

— also featuring —

When the Devil Calls
~ and ~ Vengeance

Illustrated by John R. Neill
& Douglas Hilliker
Cover by Emmett Watson

A BOLD VENTURE PRESS BOOK

These stories are presented in paperback for the first time.

The Hobo's Secret — *Railroad Stories Magazine,* October 1936

Rawhider — *Railroad Stories Magazine,* November 1936

Death Traps — *Railroad Stories Magazine,* December 1936

When the Devil Calls — *Railroad Man's Magazine,* October 1930

Vengeance — *Railroad Stories Magazine,* May 1935

RAILROAD STORIES #6
Copyright © 2019 White River Productions, Inc. All Rights Reserved.

Rich Harvey, Editor & Designer
Cover illustrations: Emmett Watson
Story Illustrations by: Douglas Hilliker ("Vengeance") and John R. Neill (all other stories)

Contents

I.
The Saga of Kiamichi Bill

The
Hobo's Secret

Chapter I

Opening Round

KIAMICHI BILL had a hunch something was going to happen that night when the local freight dragged up the grade slowly to head in at Dripping Springs. As Blackie Burns was always saying, he could "feel it in his bones."

The two men were "blanket stiffs." That is, wanderers who carry around bed blankets and sleep wherever night happens to find them. Bill was in the morning of life — young, husky, tireless. Blackie had already climbed above the ridge of middle age, where the shadows slant toward the west, but keen gray eyes showed he was still a long way from the sunset.

The pair were camping at the springs in the walnut grove a quarter-mile below the passing track switch. They had come down to the right-of-way fence that evening to watch the freight go by.

Blackie always watched the freights go by. He acted as if their rattle and creak were music to his soul. Because they fascinated him so, Bill reckoned that the old man belonged to them, had maybe given them the arm that once filled his empty sleeve.

But Blackie never discussed his past with Bill, and the latter was not too curious. Bill remembered with gratitude that the old blanket stiff had rescued him from death by smallpox in a lonely cordwood-chopper's cabin in the Kiamichi Hills, and so he did not attempt to pry into the other's secrets.

This evening, as they leaned against the barbed wires, the young hobo was aware of an eager wistfulness on the part of his companion. Blackie's mutilated right hand was stroking the empty sleeve, as he often did when he was troubled.

The laboring hog came up the hill with the head brakeman on the pilot step and the engineer leaning from his window. Trailing it were loads of cordwood, empties, merchandise peddlers, and gondolas piled high with ties hewn from the surrounding Ozarks.

The caboose trailed the loaded gondolas. A man of fifty — a *hard* conductor, if Bill knew his railroaders — was glowering down from the cupola window. A young brakeman in sateen and serge was entertaining two girls on the rear platform. One was a mere kid. The other, a redhead, who was flirting mischievously, had the kind of face and figure which wrecks empires — and sends blanket stiffs hunting jobs instead of handouts.

Kiamichi Bill didn't pay much attention to them. Not until later. He knew that the redhead flung him and Blackie a contemptuous glance, made some smart remark to the brakeman, and went on flirting.

The freight dragged up the hill. Bill returned to the fire under the bluff. For a long time the old blanket stiff leaned against the wires and stared up the track as if ghosts of dead years rode the glistening steel.

Minutes after the freight caboose had gone through the cut, he joined Bill by the bluff. He did not talk, but sat staring into the glowing embers. His comrade divided time between watching him and shying pebbles at an inquisitive jay which kept hopping down to peck at the scant remnants of their frugal meal.

When the sun had set and shade was creeping up the valley, the old man spoke, almost as if talking to himself.

"Shore is purty, ain't she?"

"Who?"

The boy stayed an upraised arm.

"Girl on the platform of old — "

"You ain't falling in love with her, are you, Blackie?" Kiamichi Bill cast the pebble at the blue jay.

"Nope." The old fellow didn't crack a smile. "Nope. I couldn't do that, son. But she shore is purty. Looks as much like …."His voice drifted off to the realm of forgotten yesterdays.

THE local freight had work in Dripping Springs. Conductor Charlie Ross told his hind brakeman:

"We'll be here two hours. You tie this rear end down good. A lot of officials out snooping around on a motor car will pass us, and they ain't going to find *my* train on this hillside with no brakes on it."

"Okay, boss," answered the brake-man, Alabama Joe Shields. "We'll wind 'em all up if you say so."

"You be damned sure you wind up plenty of 'em, smart aleck," Ross said shortly.

The boomer winked at the redheaded girl. "Your old man's kinda hostile," he muttered." Could it be the *padre* don't approve of a future railroad president makin' love to his daughter?"

"The *padre* doesn't approve of *any* man making love to his daughter," Lula Ross said saucily.

Alabama Joe fished a hickory club from under a cupola cushion and started out to set the brakes, but he didn't go.

All day seventeen-year-old Lula's hazel eyes had been flashing invitations he could not accept while papa and the annoying kid sister were in the parlor.

When the kid sister went to play with the station agent's poodle and Old Charlie went to look after the train, Alabama Joe sprang the trap on a flock of kisses.

Fifteen minutes later, he looked at his watch. He was already overdue at the merchandise peddler. He lighted his markers, forgot the brakes, and dashed madly up to unload a couple of tons of local freight.

The conductor was waiting impatiently. "Took you a helluva time to set a few brakes," he rasped.

Alabama remembered now the brakes he should have set and didn't. He smiled wisely and said, " You told me to tie down plenty of 'em."

" I didn't tell you to set them all."

Alabama didn't say he had not even anchored the caboose. Instead, he set to work and didn't let it worry him. Why should it?

Setting hand brakes on a local in a passing track was the bunk anyhow. Air brakes were on the cars. Eventually they would leak off, of course; but before they did, the boys would have finished their switching, coupled back into the train, and cut in the air.

The whole crew was busy for the next hour. The swing man, aided by a student with a cinder in his eye, sorted five loads of cordwood from the house track, cut in empties to replace them, and spotted stock cars at the pens, coal at the chute, and wheat at the mill.

Old Charlie had his time occupied herding a crew of students and boomers to see they didn't bungle things and get him into trouble.

ALABAM' was a wise boy who knew how to get things done. A gang of future railroad men had gathered at the station to watch the local come in. They always do that at evening in the little Ozark towns. Alabam' organized a crew of strong-backed volunteers to practice unloading freight.

The younger boys he told to "get the hell out of here before you get hurt!" They broke up into pairs, and while their older brothers were practicing unloading they were practicing other things.

One turned the angle-cock ahead of a gondola load of cross-ties — intending, of course, to turn it back. His pal yanked the coupling lever. It wasn't the first one he had yanked, but this time the pin came up. He took a rock and tried to knock it down, but it wouldn't go.

Fearing they had broken the thing, the lads ran away, leaving the car uncoupled and the air-brake line to the rear closed.

Ordinarily that would not have hurt a thing; but while this pair had been tampering with the couplings, another pair had been practicing with the bleed cocks on the gondolas. Bleed cocks, you know, are on brake cylinders to release set brakes. They are controlled by little levers placed directly under the center of the car.

The boys, working out of sight behind the train, opened the bleed cocks and listened to the hiss of escaping air. They had often seen brakemen do this, and it was lots of fun. When they had released all but the caboose, the kid sister, on her way back to tease Lula, heard them and shouted:

"You little devils, get away from there and let them alone!"

The "little devils" got away. The kid sister went into the caboose.

Alabam' finished unloading merchandise, and strolled over to the office. Conductor Ross was there getting orders on the motor car load of railroad officials coming up from the east and the two extras coming down from the west.

The head brakeman remained at the engine. The swing man coupled his cut of cars into the train, and cut in the air. He heard it go through, and without going back to the caboose to see whether it was showing on the gage, crossed the tracks to the restaurant for a cup of coffee.

For thirty minutes the caboose and seven heavy loads had been hanging over the hill with one brake on them. When the swing man coupled in twenty cars ahead, the jar knocked the caboose brake loose and started the cars moving. They didn't move fast, because the grade was not steep.

The girls were not alarmed. The few times they had ridden with Dad, the caboose had always been on the move; and besides they were too busy with a sisterly argument.

The kid sister was gleefully caressing a red spot on Lula's neck and crowing:

"Alabam' left a hickey on you, Lula."

"Didn't do any such a thing, fisty britches," denied the older sister.

"Did, too."

"Didn't, either."

"Look in the glass and see."

While Lula, blushing furiously, was covering the hickey with paint and powder, the caboose split the switch, and went rambling down the main line into the face of the official motorcar almost due.

OLD BLACKIE BURNS was first to come alive to what had happened. While he was staring toward town, the caboose with its green tail lights swam out of the cut, running fifteen miles an hour. He jumped up. The gray eyes widened. Although it was nearly dark, he could see beyond the loaded gondolas and see they were not coupled to an engine.

He whirled and shouted to Kiamichi Bill: "Lookut that, will yuh?"

"Lookut what?" Bill grunted listlessly. " I don't see nothing."

"Them cars! They're running away!"

"A-a-a-a, salt an' apple sauce!"

"No salt an' apple sauce about it. Them tail lights would be red instead of green if they wasn't."

Kiamichi Bill glimpsed the lights. He did not know much about railroading, but he did know that tail lights ought to be red when the tail was on the main stem.

Blackie was flopping like a trout on a spinner. "Them fellers has let them cars git away!" he cried. "They'll go in the ditch an' kill — "

Lula Ross dashed to the platform, peered around the end of the caboose and let out a war whoop. That brought the kid sister. If they had been wise, they would both have loped off into the weeds; but they had not been around the railroad enough to be wise.

They grabbed each other and began screaming: "What'll we do! Oh, what will we do!"

Blackie made a sashay at the fence with Kiamichi Bill trailing. He got tangled in the barbed wires, and could not get untangled with one piece of hand.   He screeched and bellowed:

"Ketch 'em, Kiamichi! Fer the love uh Gawd! *Ketch* 'em an' *stop* 'em!"

Kiamichi Bill was a blanket stiff, not a hero. He knew very well that if he were on that string of cars he would fall all over himself getting off. But Bill loved old Blackie as only a youth can who has been saved from death, taught of life, and led out to the far places. For six years he and Blackie had suffered, sinned, and rejoiced together; and Bill had followed blindly.

The young hobo reached for the top wire — but he didn't reach too fast. Memory was flashing visions of that wreck out on the Espee last summer where twenty runaway cars had gone off a mountain and pinned a poor bum underneath to burn alive. He and Blackie had been too close to that for comfort.

He watched the cars. They were gaining headway. He turned back and started to protest. But Blackie was pleading; and when the caboose was a hundred yards away, he could see Lula Ross, with hands outstretched, hear her terrified voice imploring him: "Save us! Oh, mister, save us! We'll be killed!"

STOUT as a bull and quick as a kitten, Bill placed a gnarled hand on the post, leaped the fence, and met the caboose as it came on.

The conductor's daughter did not fall on his neck when he stumbled up the caboose steps. If she had, he would probably have tumbled off and run for the woods.

Bill caught the brake wheel and commenced to wind it. She hurried into the caboose, with one protecting arm around the kid sister, and brought out the club which Alabama Joe had

failed to use.

Kiamichi Bill was awkward, but he soon had the caboose buckling over a well-set brake. He hurried to the gondolas. When they had run a mile, brakes were on all the cars and soon they had stopped midway a straight stretch of track halfway to Skunk Creek.

The youth has grown up to fear women. A snuff-dipping stepmother had used to kick his pants and burn him up with hickory switches. He felt a strong urge to flee up to the protection of Blackie Burns, but a stronger one drew him down to the rear — and to the rear he went.

The girls were dancing around on a sand bar beside the track, chattering excitedly about their close call. If they had even known of the motorcar behind them, it was now forgotten.

Red-haired Lula met her rescuer at the forward platform. In

the one glance he stole at her, he knew she was ravishingly beautiful.

Tears of gratitude glistening in her big hazel eyes and clinging to the soft lashes started something growing inside of him — something which paralyzed his tongue and left him standing there ashamed as Adam was in Eden's garden.

His eyes fell; and he became suddenly aware that his ragged suit was patched with flour sack, that his hands were cracked and soiled and his nails broken, that his hair was long and his face dirty and unshaven.

Into that awareness, while he debated whether to touch the soft, outstretched hand with his own filthy one, came the rapid *put—put—t-t-t* of a motorcar racing up the hill. It stopped ten feet from the tail hose with two green lights shining over; and seven "brass hats" (officials) came tumbling out, led by the division superintendent, smoking a long cigar and sternly demanding to know why that caboose was on the main stem without a flag.

Kiamichi Bill did not do the explaining. He left that to the conductor's daughter. While she talked, he drew circles in the sand with the brake club and tried to hide three dirty toes peeping through a crack in that old shoe he had salvaged from a trash can in a little town in Iowa.

Vaguely he heard her speak of "This — this young gentleman," and a long time afterward knew she had been referring to him.

"If it had not been for his bravely catching these cars and stopping them," she said to the tall superintendent, "we would all surely have been dead by now."

"You're telling me!" the super rasped. And then he turned to Kiamichi Bill.

All his life, the young hobo had been cuffed and chased about by railroaders until he had come to fear and almost hate them. When, however, he looked timidly into the face of Superintendent

King Lawson, hate and fear were gone, and he thrilled to the bass voice saying:

"You've done us a good turn tonight, boy. If there's anything we can do for you — "

"We can pass the hat and buy him a suit of clothes," interrupted a clerk impulsively.

"We owe him something — "

THE blast of an engine whistle split the twilight silence. It was up the hill toward Dripping Springs, but it wasn't standing still.

The others stared unconcernedly. Superintendent Lawson let out a roar, hit for the head end running as fast as his long legs would carry him, and shouting over his shoulder:

"Get out of the way, folks! That's old Charlie Ross comin' after his hind end. He'll be runnin' a million miles an hour. Look out! They're goin' to hit!"

The motor engineer started the doodlebug toward Skunk Creek. The brass hats headed for the timber. The girls and Kiamichi Bill followed.

The engine came out of the cut backing up. King Lawson swung them a stop sign. Men tumbled off it. It rammed the gondolas with a cannon roar. Dust fogged the atmosphere. Echoes whispered among the trees.

At length the commotion subsided. The cars were all together. Alabama Joe let off the brakes which Bill had set, and they all returned to Dripping Springs.

The girls told wide-eyed townsfolk of the thrilling ride and daring rescue. Officials asked prying questions. Old Charlie swore he had instructed the hind brakeman to set brakes on the rear end. Alabama swore with equal firmness that he had set every brake as tight as he could wind them.

Lawson, instead of telling Alabama what kind of liar he was, suggested that cars didn't run out of side tracks with brakes on them, and made a date with the whole crew in his office the following morning at nine o'clock.

When the super had gone to look over the train, the conductor came to Kiamichi Bill with the pencil and the book. The young hobo glanced from him to his daughter and mentally reckoned the girl didn't get her good looks from the old man.

A cauliflower ear, a sunken place in the center of the forehead that would hold half an English walnut, and a twisted nose gave him the appearance of the meanest man that ever kicked a blanket stiff out of a box car.

"What's yuh name, *'bo?'*" He emphasized the *'bo.*

It had been so long since the youth had used a name that he had to think a minute. Finally he answered: "Burns — William Burns," adding, "Blackie calls me Kiamichi Bill."

"Burns! Blackie!"

Kiamichi Bill did not like the vicious ring of the conductor's echo.

"Yeah. Burns. B-u-r-n-s. That's my name. If it ain't good enough — "

The conductor had glanced guiltily around to see if he had been heard. Apparently he had not.

In lower tone, he growled: "That's all right, 'bo. All I need it for's to report to the office."

WHILE excitement had reigned, Blackie Burns, nursing barbed wire cuts and skinned shins, had joined the group. He was within arm's reach of the conductor when Old Charlie finished writing the name.

The minute the conductor looked up, Bill sensed that Blackie and Ross had met before. The conductor's black eyes flared wide, as if he had seen a ghost, and narrowed quickly to bits of obsidian.

They looked at each other while the watch ticked off ninety seconds. Neither of them said a word. Finally, Blackie shuffled away and disappeared behind a pile of ties. The conductor stalled around, went into the caboose, and came out wiping his mouth on a jumper sleeve. After a while he, too, disappeared behind the pile of ties.

The other officials followed Superintendent Lawson toward the office. The girls returned to their caboose. Only Kiamichi Bill remained, leaning against the side of the gondola, waiting for Blackie and the conductor to end their conference. Lawson came back from the head end and stopped beside him, and said:

"We sure are indebted to you, boy. The fellows asked me to give you this."

He passed out a wad of bills.

"Why, mister," the young blanket stiff protested. "I — I wasn't — doin' it for — "

"Yeah, I know."

The superintendent grinned affably as Bill fingered the money. Although it was not much, it represented more than the youth had ever owned before in his life.

"I — I'm sure obliged to you, mister," he faltered.

"That's all right, kid. You had it comin'."

Bill put the gift into a pocket, remembered the pocket had holes, and took them out. Lawson kept watching covertly. He laid a hand on a ragged shoulder and said quietly: "You'd make a good railroad man, boy."

"Think so?" Kiamichi Bill glowed. It was the first time anybody except Blackie Burns had ever suggested he might be good at anything.

"Sure. You'd like it, too."

"Blackie says it's the nearest to muh present occupation of anything he knows of," Bill chuckled.

The super eyed him quizzically and asked: "Blackie who?"

"Blackie Burns. He's my pal."

Lawson said: "Oh, I see."

An extra freight came down the hill and headed into the passing track. The *Oklahoma Mail* came up from the east and stormed away toward Tulsa. Still neither blanket stiff nor conductor came from behind that the pile.

Bill shuffled uneasily. The freight backed out and came down the main, and when it had run, Charlie Ross emerged, went into his caboose, and sat at the table.

The motorcar eased down toward the switch. Lawson was going toward it. He turned and called to Kiamichi Bill:

"Think about that job, kid, and look me up in Springvale."

"I shore will, an' much obliged for the dough!"

THE motor *put-putted* up the main line. The local eased out of siding and followed it. Blackie Burns shuffled from the shadows and in silence led the way toward the camp in the walnut grove.

Hours later, the youth told of Superintendent Lawson's suggestion. He asked a little wistfully:

"Yuh goin' to do it?"

"Somethin' seems to tell me — "

"Yeah, I know. I seen it this evenin'. It's that redheaded girl of — of his."

"N-no," Bill stammered. "'Tain't that. I — yuh see, Blackie, I been think-in' fer a long time mebbe I oughta get me a job an' have a home like other folks, an' fix up a place fer you — "

"Listen, Kiamichi," Blackie interrupted. "You ain't foolin' me none. Jist one thing puts thoughts like that into a young feller's head — an' that one thing's a *woman*. I ain't object-in' nor criticizin'."

"But I don't even know — why that filly wouldn't even wipe her feet — "

"Quit a kiddin' yourself, Kiamichi. I been figgerin' a long

time this was comin'. I'm glad — glad. You go right on an' take
that job, an' you'll never be sorry fer it."

"I'll think about it, Blackie."

"Don't think about it. *Do it!*"

Long the two blanket stiffs sat by their fire that night. Six
years they had rambled together up and down the far-flung steel.
Each owed much to the other. Even before Bill had talked, they
had seemed to know that they would never spend another night
together until they camped beside those fires not made by hand
in the last great Jungle.

II

Rawhiding a Student Brakeman

BARBER and clothier worked a wonderful transformation in
Kiamichi Bill. He went into Lawson's office cleaned and well
clad, but scared grinless.

"I scarcely knew you, kid," King Lawson said with an approv-
ing nod.

"Reckon I do look different," Bill returned with a proud glance
over the first store suit he had ever worn.

"Yes, you do." The superintendent lighted a cigar and offered
one to Kiamichi Bill. Clothes," he said significantly, "may not
make a gentleman, but they do make a devil of a lot of difference
in a *man's* appearance."

Bill agreed he was right.

"Looking for that job?" the super queried.

"Yes — yes, sir, if you still — "

"I figured you would," Lawson said. "What line you going
into?"

"Sir?"

"I mean, what kind of job do you want? Train service? Engine
service? Yard service? Shops? Roundhouse? You see, there are

all kinds of jobs around a railroad."

The ex-hobo required little time for decision. As a small boy he had seen brakemen riding comfortably in cab and cupola, or dangling well-shod feet against sides of box cars. Then he had envied them.

Six years he had been chased and kicked by them while he stole rides on their freights, and he had grown to covet their position as lords of the side-door Pullman. Yesterday he had seen one dressed in sateen and serge, making love to the girl of his dreams, and she had seemed to like it.

"Where," he asked wistfully, "does a 'bo start in to be a brakeman?"

"Where? As student brakeman on the local."

"Do you mean I can start in right now?"

"Sure," said Lawson. "If you want to be a brakeman, I'll send you out with the local conductor. You'll have to work without pay until you get onto the ropes. You've got to learn to handle yourself on the train, learn the road and the stations, learn signals and how to give and receive them, and learn the rules. When the local conductor okays you, you're marked up on the extra board, and go making trips when the regular men lay off."

That sounded easy. Kiamichi Bill emerged from the office treading air. Already he could see himself riding freights with nobody to kick him off, drawing big pay checks, buying ice cream sodas, and flirting with the dames, particularly the redhead with big hazel eyes and the softest hand he had ever touched.

He even tried to imagine himself standing on a caboose platform, with her looking up into his eyes and fixing the red silk tie, as she had been doing that day with Alabama Joe.

ALL that Saturday and Sunday when he was not trying to accustom himself to sleeping in a room on a bed with springs and a mattress and white sheets, the future brakeman was strutting around town in his ten-dollar store suit with his head in the clouds.

When he presented himself to old Charlie Ross on Monday morning, he dropped abruptly to earth.

The conductor was on the warpath, ready, as the boys who knew him would say, to throw a fit. Although he despised students, Lawson had kept from one to three on his crew all summer and fall.

Moreover, though the investigation had not held him responsible for the escape of the cars from Dripping Springs, the super had told him and Alabama Joe things they would not forget until the day they put on their wooden kimonos.

Even that, however, did not account for the viciousness of his attack on Kiamichi Bill. It began when the boy offered the letter from Lawson.

"I know!" he roared. "That knuckle-headed wampus cat sent you down here for me to make a brakeman out of — you, a lousy, filthy, back-door-hittin' blanket stiff! Well, it can't be done. You ain't no brakeman, an' you never will be, an' I don't aim to try it."

Kiamichi Bill gasped and turned white. Alabama Joe grinned and winked at Lazy Lou, the big swing man.

Ross, his disfigured face distorted in a snarl of hate, his voice shaking with passion, continued:

"What does he think this is? Reform school or somethin'? Damn his soul, if he wants to pick up scum from the hobo jungles an' make 'em into railroaders, he can get somebody else to do it. I won't. Do you hear me, I *won't* do it! You take this letter back to him, and tell him to — "

In burning words of one syllable, the conductor told Kiamichi Bill what Lawson could do with the letter, and told him a lot of other things.

The youth started dazedly toward the office. Never since his snuff-dipping stepmother had kicked his pants off for letting the pet coon fall in the ash barrel while she was drunk had he had such a berating. When he was two car-lengths away, Ross roared after him:

"Where'n hell you think you're go-in' ?"

"You told me — "

"Come back here, idiot! Think you'll go blabberin' to that cock-eyed fool, an' have him fire me? Come back here, I say! Get in this caboose an' stay here till I tell you to get out."

Thus began Kiamichi Bill's initiation. If he had known where to find Blackie Burns that morning while he waited for the men to make their train, he would have given up and gone back to the hobo trail.

But he did not know. The old stiff, never anxious to say good-by, had sneaked out of the camp at Dripping Springs in the night, had hooked a freight, and gone without a hint of his destination.

BECAUSE Bill knew his old pal could not be found, because the lingering touch of King Lawson's reassuring hand was ever on his shoulder, and because a pair of hazel eyes kept beckoning, he remained to fight it through.

For three weeks the rawhiding continued. Old Charlie rarely spoke except to snarl or bellow; and as the days went by his hatred seemed to increase rather than to diminish. He vented his spleen on the other fellows, and they in turn took it out on the student.

Although other students carried lanterns and were treated with some consideration, they ignored Kiamichi Bill or treated him as an outcast. They didn't even move over to offer him sitting room on the cushions.

When they were switching, they forgot he was around anxious to learn; but when the water barrel was empty, it was:

"Hi, you stiff! Fill up this water barrel when we stop at the creek, an' don't you spill it all over the floor."

When there was freight to unload, one of them, usually Alabama Joe — who seemed to hold Bill responsible for the bawling out Lawson had given him — would call:

"Hi, bo! We need a strong back an' a weak mind over here at the peddler. Come on!"

And the others would laugh. Then the man who was breaking out saw to it the heavy pieces, the filthy pieces, the rough pieces, went to Kiamichi Bill.

But the youth never whimpered, never cheeped to Lawson when they met. He might have gone on learning nothing until his dwindling funds gave out, or until he grew discouraged and quit. That was probably what Old Charlie hoped for … but the affair at Skunk Creek brought a change.

Whether that deal was hatched up among the crew, or whether it was the result of devilish impulse born of hate and malice, Bill never knew.

It was Saturday of his third week, and he was pretty much discouraged, because he knew he was net learning the things he should have learned. The local was held in Oldberg two hours that morning waiting for merchandise from the east. That put them out late, and with the heavy Saturday switching, they lost time all day long.

It was late afternoon when they pulled into Skunk Creek. With no trains due, they stopped on the main line. Both the head brakeman and the fireman were clamoring to eat. The engineer carried a lunch. Old Charlie wasn't hungry.

"Student an' me will do the switching while you boys go fill up," he said.

That should have warned Kiamichi Bill to be on his guard, because Old Charlie spoke with the nearest approach to friendliness he had ever used, and winked at Alabama Joe when he said it.

BILL misread the signal. Rejoicing that at last he was going to learn to switch cars, he cut ahead of the two merchandise, bled the air off the head end and took it over into the house track as directed.

There was a pretty stiff grade to the east through Skunk Creek, enough so that cars didn't need a kick to get them moving. Bill had noticed that when Lazy Lou was switching, he took the slack, pulled the pin, and let them roll back to the head man, Eddie Summers. Even then they got plenty of speed in the quarter mile from the house track switch down to the station.

"I'll cut 'em off to you an' you anchor 'em," the conductor said shortly.

That was what Bill had expected. He said, "Okay, Mr. Ross."

"You'll have to step lively now," warned the old grouch. "Don't let 'em git away from you an' tear hell out of something."

"I'll do my best, sir."

The first cut brought ten empty flat cars on the train. Ross let them come pretty slow. Kiamichi Bill stopped them even with the station. The conductor threw the switch and cut off two empty stock cars in the house track.

An experienced man would have observed that those cars had been taken from the stock chutes and had to go back there. Bill had not noticed and did not know. As he came running up the house track to meet them, the conductor stuck thumbs in ears and wigwagged outspread palms.

Although that signal is not in the rule book, an experienced man would have understood it as "Spot them at the stock chutes." Kiamichi Bill didn't understand. The rule book did not give that signal; the men had never told him. He rode them almost to the end of the track and tied them down.

By the time he had them anchored, Ross was bringing the

whole head end down the house track. He coupled into the two stock cars. He was roaring like a bull elephant fed cayenne pepper.

"Why'n hell didn't you spot them cars back at the chutes?"

"I didn't know — "

"Naw, you don't know anything! You never will. I told you you'd never be a brakeman. You'd better git your filthy rags an' your tin cans an' go back with — Git up there an' let off them brakes. See if you can do that without a conductor havin' to climb up an' show you how."

Kiamichi Bill made other blunders. Ross gave other outlaw signals, and stormed and raved when he did not understand them. As the work progressed, he kept kicking a little harder and a little harder, until by the time the job was finished, Bill was fairly racing from one track to the other to keep them from hitting.

ABOUT sundown they finished. The crew had now come back from supper. They coupled the train, which now consisted of the caboose, two merchandise peddlers, and twenty flat cars ahead of them. Old Charlie smirked when they finally met at the merchandise car to do their unloading.

Alabam' asked jokingly: "How did you like your new brakeman, Charlie?"

"He sure catches 'em on the fly. You ought to take lessons from him."

The rawhider winked at the big swing man. Alabam' broke the seal on the merchandise car and gave it to the agent. Ross turned to Kiamichi Bill and said:

"If you want to eat, 'bo, you better run over to the beanery. Me an' the boys will unload the freight."

Kiamichi Bill was glowing with pride in achievement. He figured the efficiency with which he had handled the field job had softened the conductor's hard heart. He looked at the dollar watch, which he had bought while studenting.

"How long will we be here?" he asked.

Ross glanced at his own watch. There was a sly grin under the twisted nose.

"Fifteen minutes, at least. We've got to unload this freight an' take water."

The water tank was at the east end of the passing track, a quarter mile below the station. Usually the head brakeman cut off the engine and ran through the passing track while the others were unloading freight. Tonight the head brakeman was at the peddler car.

That should have aroused the student's suspicion, but it didn't. He was hungry. He ran over to the restaurant, which stood back to the railroad, and ordered a couple of eggs. While eating them, he heard the engine start. He did not notice that the train started, too.

Soon he finished supper and walked around the end of the restaurant. The train was not in sight. Bill hurried to the station platform. He saw that instead of cutting off the engine and going light for water, they had backed the whole train down below the tank. They whistled off and started moving. He went striding down the platform to meet them.

He did not try to catch the engine. She went by him running twenty miles an hour. The three men were all peering down at him as she roared by. Bill looked up at them, extended his hands with palms up, and shook them. That, he had learned by watching, was the signal the conductor gave when he wanted to catch the caboose.

The men let out a yell. The engineer grabbed the whistle cord and sent out a long-drawn *whoo-whooooaaah!* telling the world he was leaving Skunk Creek, and leaving plenty fast;

Three lighted lanterns on the rear swung the high sign in answer to his signal.

THAT'S when Kiamichi Bill realized he had been tricked, knew Charlie Ross intended to leave him at Skunk Creek and let him walk in. He gasped at the flat cars streaming past. He knew he would not dare try to catch them. Nobody ever catches flat cars when they're running fast, because the grab-irons are not made for catching.

He gave a "stop" sign. The hind end gave a "go ahead." The engineer whistled again, and kept hammering the old teakettle for all she was worth, picking up speed with the light train on the grade.

Most students would have backed off from those cars and let them go. But Kiamichi Bill had not spent six years riding freight trains without learning some things about them. Though he had never caught one running that fast, he thought he could. He let the twenty flats go by. They were doing close to thirty — twenty-five, at least.

Loafers on the station platform were watching. The agent was watching. On the hotel platform, somebody else was watching, but Kiamichi Bill didn't know it. He stood close to the train with arms dangling at his sides, gaging its speed.

The first high car was a reefer with good ladder and wide stirrup. When it came on, he started ahead of it.

The loafers gasped. The agent yelled. Grins froze on the faces of three trainmen who had been trying to pull a fast one. A voice from the hotel veranda shouted:

"Don't do that! Let it go! You'll be killed!"

Kiamichi Bill didn't hear the voice. Probably nobody else did. He raced for forty feet ahead of the car. When it came on, he gripped the grab-irons, and leaped for the stirrup.

His foot struck it, and glanced off. For a hundred feet he dangled alongside, holding by his arms. Unconsciously, Conductor Ross had gripped the conductor's valve and emptied the train line. As the brakes took hold, Bill found the stirrup with the good right foot, climbed safely to the top of the reefer, and went in through the cupola window.

Old Charlie had come out of his trance and started swearing. The brakemen were not laughing. Bill climbed over their feet, dropped to the floor, and took a sip of ice water. Neither of them spoke to him while the brakes were pumping off, nor while they were working on into Springvale.

ON Sunday morning, King Lawson had the local conductor in the office and said casually:

"Called you in to see how the new student's getting along, Mr. Ross?"

The conductor's mouth came shut like a trap and the hole in the forehead turned from bronze to crimson.

"You mean that blanket stiff?"

"I mean Blackie Burns's kid."

Ross stared out through the window where leaves on the sycamore and maple were turning yellow.

"Washout, Mr. Lawson — a reg'lar washout."

"You mean he's no good?" Lawson parried.

"Sure. He's no brakeman an' never will be. All the conductors in the States an' Canada couldn't make one out of him."

Lawson drawled: "Seemed to be doing a pretty good job handling those cars you cut off to him last night at Skunk Creek."

Conductor Ross suddenly looked worried, but he didn't say anything.

The official continued: "You see, Mr. Ross, I was there between trains yesterday trying to straighten out the tangle over the new grade crossing. I saw you cutting off those cars to him at a rate you'd never dare cut them off to that regular head man of yours. I also heard you tearing into him when he didn't catch that stock chute signal you handed him."

"Did you?" said the conductor.

"Yes." Lawson nodded. "Another thing, Mr. Ross. I'd like for you to explain why you tried to leave him at Skunk Creek last night."

"I didn't — "

"Don't lie to me, sir. I know you did, and you came damn near committing a murder. Listen, Ross. I know there's something back of this. You hate that kid. I can see it in your eye. What's wrong?"

Ross hemmed and hawed.

Superintendent Lawson kept insisting. "You might as well come clean with me. I want to know what's the trouble between you and him."

"He's a lousy bum," the old skipper said at length. "I don't like the idea of teaching bums to railroad."

"Oh, you don't, eh?"

"No, I don't."

Lawson pierced the conductor with cold, blue-gray eyes. "That's funny. If some guy kept my daughters from being mashed into a jelly in a tail-end collision, I'd be falling all over myself trying to be nice — "

"That thing was framed, Mr. Lawson," the conductor snarled.

"Framed?"

"Yeah. Framed. Them two bums let the brakes off my rear end an' then pretended — "

"You know that's not so, Ross. Your own daughters say they were at the fence when the caboose came down. Besides, why should they?"

Ross looked away and muttered:

"Quien sabe? (Who knows?)" He had nothing else to say.

***

III

Old Charlie's Ultimatum

LAWSON was a wise official. He did not press the matter further. He knew he was not going to learn anything from the conductor. He dismissed Ross and called in Kiamichi Bill.

"How's the job coming, kid?" he queried.

"Okay, Mr. Lawson."

"You and Ross getting along all right?" He eyed the boy keenly.

"Sure!" said Bill.

Lawson chuckled. His kind admire the man who can swallow a raw deal without gagging. He waited a minute and came directly to the point.

"I'd like to get a little information if you can give it," he said.

"Sure. Anything — "

"This pal of yours, this Blackie — what was his other name?"

"Burns. Blackie Burns."

"Burns, huh!" Lawson frowned. "Where'd he come from? What'd he do before he went hoboing?"

"First time I ever saw him," said Bill, "was down in the Kiamichi Mountains of eastern Oklahoma six years ago. My folks all died of smallpox, and I had it, too. Blackie come in and nursed me through, and I went bummin' with him. All I know is, he was the best pal a man ever had."

Lawson nodded. "Do you know whether he ever worked on a railroad?"

Bill wondered if Blackie was in trouble.   He decided not.

"I'm not sure, Mr. Lawson," he answered slowly, "but from

the way he acted when he watched the trains run, and the way he hung around the railroads, I figured maybe he had. Why?"

The brass hat shrugged. "I've been kind of curious ever since he and Ross hid out up there that night at Dripping Springs."

"Did you notice that?"

" I couldn't help it."

"You think — "

" I think there's something between those two, and I've got a hunch that's why Ross has been rawhiding hell out of you these last three weeks."

Bill said, " Oh!" and grinned sheepishly.

Lawson continued: "A guy named Blackie worked here when Ross first came. He was killed in a wreck."

"Killed in a wreck! Then it couldn't be — "

"I wasn't working here then," Lawson interrupted. "But I heard about it since I came. It seems this Blackie — Blackie McCallam his name was — and Ross hired out braking here about the same time. McCallam was a regular booze hound. Before they had been here a week, he got drunk and he and Ross had a devil of a fight. Before they were through with it, they were called, McCallam to flag on first Number Thirty-six, and Ross to break ahead on the second one."

The youth was listening intently.

Lawson went on: "Down on the hill below Dripping Springs, if I get it right, something happened to first Thirty-six. McCallam, probably drunk in the caboose — nobody ever did know for certain — didn't go back flagging. The second train came down that hill a thousand miles an hour, and sloughed into 'em. That's where Charlie Ross got the hole in his head, and the broken nose and the silver wires in his jaws."

"Oh!" Kiamichi Bill studied a minute. He remembered how Blackie Burns, though the S. &'S. had been their shortest route from coast to coast, had always shunned it until this last trip. "And you think Blackie Burns is McCallam?"

"I did at first, but I've decided it couldn't be. McCallam's body was identified, and the insurance company paid his widow, who lives in Ohio. No, it's something else."

"Is queer, though, about those two."

"Yes. Lots of queer things happen around a railroad."

LAWSON gave Kiamichi Bill a pass that evening and sent him to Oldberg to finish his student trips with Seth Bailey's crew.

"Bailey's a good man," he said. "He'll give you a break, and you'll find life a little different."

Bill did not regret the change. Bailey was an inveterate kidder, always playing pranks and having his fun, but he was no rawhide. On a tip from Lawson he gave the boy some special bits of attention, and within the month had him on the extra board drawing pay.

The next few months were unsettled ones. The first months in any brake-man's life are unsettled. There is a lack of comradeship, a dearth of social life in terminal, and a feeling that the other fellows are either laughing or scoffing at one's ignorance.

Kiamichi Bill learned rapidly. Though he had been but little in school, could scarcely write or even read, his years roughing it with Blackie Burns had given him the ability to observe and to imitate.

Soon he knew how to get drawbars to make a coupling, how to snap, hose connections with a quick flip of the wrists, how to cool a hot box, or change its packing, or slip in a brass if need be.

He learned also to run for switches on the grade, where he should work in doubling hills, and in switching house tracks, and in switching around curves where he had to pass signals from the rear end.

He made trips with almost every crew on the district. Some men encouraged him. Others treated him contemptuously, as if they could never forget he had been a hobo.

Often, as they roared by the local freight in siding, he would see Charlie Ross on the caboose platform or striding the station, or out chasing hoboes.

Although Ross had been no different from other conductors until Kiamichi Bill had come, it was whispered that the very sight of a bum riding his trains turned him into a regular maniac. Men who worked for Ross declared he would dash out into the rain bareheaded and in his shirt sleeves to kick or club them off, no matter how fast the train was running.

The old conductor never spoke to Kiamichi Bill, never lifted a hand. He acted as if, by ignoring the young brakeman, he could blot out memory of things best forgotten. Once only did the ex-hobo get a call for Ross's crew. It was in the spring, and the head man had been hurt by a fall from a box car.

"Reckon the old wart will let me brake for him?" he asked the caller.

"He'll have to unless you do something to get fired for," was the answer.

Kiamichi Bill, though entitled to hold the turn for thirty days, made only one round trip. It was the most uncomfortable two days he had spent since he had left their car in the fall.

Ross, Alabama, Lazy Lou — none of them had forgotten those three weeks' rawhiding they had given him nor the night they had tried to leave him at the switch at Skunk Creek. When he had signed the register in Springvale, Charlie Ross was at his elbow. The round hole in his forehead was crimson, and the disfigured face was unsmiling.

"You going to hold your rights on this car?" he asked coldly.

"Not if I can get out of it."

"You can sure'n the devil get out of it. Hi, Jack — " He signaled for the caller. The youth came to the window. "This — this brakeman says he wants to mark back on the extra board and let you call somebody else on my crew."

"What about it, Burns?" the caller asked.

"Right," Bill answered. "Next time I'm first out when he's got a vacancy, call somebody else."

"Okay, if that's the way you feel about it."

Kiamichi Bill let another man take the vacancy, but that did not keep him and Ross apart.

DURING his first winter, the brakeman did well financially. He had good clothes and wore them like a prince. Girls in the restaurants noticed him, lingered when they brought his order, and a night, when business was slack and he was eating alone, they used to lean over the counter to chat with him.

He began stepping out with them, no one in particular, taking in shows and dances. Occasionally he met Lula Ross. Usually she was with Alabama Joe, who was pretty much of a lady's man; but often she was with other road men, or with young fellows from town. She always had a nod and a smile for him, but he never became really acquainted with her until summer.

There was a railroad picnic at Dripping Springs. The company ran excursion trains from division points bringing together the usual crowd of railroad men, their sisters, wives, and sweethearts. Kiamichi Bill did not lay off for it, but he was called to work one of the trains.

Although it was Sunday, Charlie Ross did not attend. Gossip said he never went anywhere except to work — super-sensitive about his disfigured features. As a consequence, Mrs. Ross managed the social life of her brood, which consisted of Lula, the kid sister, and nine-year-old twins.

Bill saw her for the first time when he came through her car opening vents. She was a queenly matron in her forties. Silky white hair crowned a sad, sweet face in which the afterglow of dazzling loveliness still lingered.

Bill knew right away whence came the daughter's beauty. Knowing how her husband felt toward him, and expecting her to hold the same feeling, the former blanket stiff was shy and awkward and did not know quite what to say when Lula introduced him.

Mrs. Ross smiled and said: "My daughter often speaks of you. She says a guardian angel must have put you and your partner on guard there that night to protect her. I've wanted to meet you and thank you personally."

"It — wasn't — wasn't anything, Mrs. Ross," Bill stammered in confusion. "Really, it wasn't."

The train disgorged its load at the grove a half-mile below where he and Blackie had had their camp that September night. The crew put their train in the siding at Dripping Springs and walked back to the grounds.

Bill mingled with other young folk, swimming, boating, riding the wooden ponies, throwing confetti, getting in the game with a rubber return ball to become acquainted with girls who looked lonely. He tried to have a good time but he did not succeed too well.

He kept thinking of Blackie Burns. He always thought of Blackie when he saw Lula Ross. He wondered where the old blanket stiff had gone, and why he had not returned this spring as he had promised. Tiring finally of the crowd, Bill found a woods path leading up to the little spring where their camp had been.

When he came around the point of rocks into the walnut grove, he stopped abruptly. Mrs. Ross and her redheaded daughter were sitting under the trees where he and Blackie had sat that last night.

Bill excused himself and started backing away, but Mrs. Ross arose hastily and said;

"No, no! Don't go. Come and join us. We grew tired of the noise and the clatter and came up here to rest. Lula wanted to show me the place where — you know — "

Lula, although far from timid, blushed confusedly. Bill sat on the grass and they talked, and Mrs. Ross asked questions. She wanted to know about "This — this partner of yours — this Blackie person."

Bill told her as much as he knew. "What kind of man was he?" she asked. "What did he look like?"

Bill grinned ruefully. "I'm afraid you would not think he was much to look at, Mrs. Ross. Right arm cut off — crippled in the other hand — grizzled beard not always clean. No, he wasn't much to look at, but … "

KIAMICHI BILL returned to the grounds with them. He and Lula rode the wooden horses and danced a square dance, and came to sit in the shade with her mother.

Alabama Joe kept watching them. When he could tear himself away from a group with whom he had been frolicking, he joined them, but did not remain long. He nodded coldly to Kiamichi, eyed Mrs. Ross hastily, and led Lula away to the dance pavilion.

Before they parted, Mrs. Ross again expressed her gratitude to Bill for his service to her daughters and extended a dinner invitation. Bill would have given a lot to accept, because he felt the winds of heaven blowing through his soul when he was near Lula, but he kept thinking about the conductor, and how bitterly the old man despised him. He stalled and made excuses.

Mrs. Ross patted his arm and said laughing: "You can't say no, sir. We'll make it Wednesday evening, if you're in. How about it?"

Bill used his head. He knew Old Charlie was at the other end of the road Wednesday evenings; and he had a hunch that Mrs. Ross remembered it, too. With an uncomfortable feeling inside of him, he accepted and managed to be in town to keep the engagement.

After that dinner there were others — always when Old Charlie was away from home. Bill, though he returned again and again, was never quite comfortable. He soon realized there was no harmony in the family. He sensed that Lula was not her father's favorite and her life was not happy.

Listening in the town, he heard rumors. It was whispered that years ago, they had lived in the East; that there had been estrangement; that two years after the accident which had disfigured Ross and had so nearly cost his life, he had brought her and their one child to Springvale where the others had been born.

How much was fact, how much fiction, he did not know; but from the very first, he felt a tension in the air, an atmosphere of mystery and of unseen tragedy stalking grimly through their lives.

Ross must have known his daughter and the former young blanket stiff were more to each other than mere casual acquaintances. Everybody else did. Although she still kept company with Alabama Joe, and Bill stepped out with bean'ry queens, the two were often together. He even called for her and took her home when the old man was there, but he was never challenged.

At the end of two years, he had become pretty well established in Springvale. He was a steady, reliable brake-man; and when business boomed the second fall, he went to work as parlor man for "Bunny" Shields. He fixed up the caboose with a bed and an oil stove, and went eating and sleeping in it and saving his money, nobody ever asked what for.

WHEN spring came, however, a passenger crew was pulled off. The conductor bumped Ross off the local; and that left Old Charlie to bump the youngest man holding a regular job, who was Bunny Shields.

Folks in the know figured there would be trouble with Kiam-ichi Bill holding the rear end. Superintendent Lawson must have thought the same thing, for the day Ross signed for the run, he hunted Bill up and said:

"You'd better watch your step, kid. Unless I miss my guess, a brakeman's scalp's going to start slipping right shortly."

"Do you think so?"

"Yeah, I sure do," Lawson responded breezily. "Whatever that man had against you when you came here, he's not lost it; and you've not helped matters by making love to that Cleopatra of his."

Bill guessed they were right. He knew that although the conductor could do him no bodily harm nor take his job away, it might soon become so unpleasant he would be forced to quit the parlor job and go riding the smoky end.

It made him hot under the collar; because he had spent money fixing the caboose, and the dollar a day saving in expenses was not to be sneezed at.

As luck would have it, Bill unwittingly left himself open to attack the day Ross came on the car. Last trip with Bunny Shields, they caught the Shriners' Special, going to convention, and their caboose was thrown on the rear. This special, instead of running into the freight yards, went into the passenger station, five miles across town at 1.40 a.m.

Always Bill pulled in his markers, stowed them away, put things to rights, and swept the caboose before leaving. But it was raining that night. The regular street cars had knocked off, and only the "owl" was running. As they were pulling in the clear, he saw the night car coming down the boulevard. He knew that if he missed it, he would either have to walk home, wait another hour, or hire a taxi.

He jerked the markers from their sockets, set them inside the rear door, blew out the lamp, locked the doors and loped off to catch the "owl," intending to get out early in the morning and clean the caboose before Ross had time to get down.

He was at the caboose by eight o'clock, but the thing looked as if the imps of hard luck had staged a wild party and forgotten to clean their mess. The yard crew bringing it over from the south side had given it a terrific jolt. The lid was off the water barrel, puddles were in the floor, mud of yesterday had turned to loblolly, and stationery had fallen into it.

Worst of all, the markers which he had set inside the door had been upset and had skidded, spilling their oil for half the length of the caboose floor.

BILL did not hunt the yardmaster and express his opinion of switchmen in general and the Springvale bunch in particular. There would be time for that after he had cleaned the caboose; but before he even started, Ross came clumping in. The old man stopped and choked and sputtered. The hole in his head became a crimson sink.

"Is — is this the way you keep a caboose?" His tone was not loud but it was dagger-sharp.

Kiamichi Bill remembered it was no use to explain, that friends understand without it, and others never believe it anyhow.   He did not reply.

The conductor continued: "That's exactly what I'd expect of a blanket stiff raised in a hobo jungle. I told you you'd never be a brakeman, and now I know it. You clean this mess out of here, and if I ever come into this caboose and find it looking like this again, I'm goin' to turn you in to your good friend Lawson and tell him to send me a brakeman."

Bill wondered why he took that, because he was learning to talk back to the hard ones; but take it he did. He scrubbed the floor from front bumper to tail house.

Ross built a stationery cabinet and arranged his stuff to suit himself as a man should do in his own private car.

He didn't speak to Bill that day nor for many days to come. Neither did he begin that rawhiding which others had predicted, and Bill had expected. The young brakeman began to wonder why, to ask himself if the old fellow could be softening on account of Mrs. Ross and Lula. But his unasked question was soon answered.

When Ross had been on the car two weeks, Bill had a date with Lula. He went boldly up the front steps and rang the doorbell. To his amazement, the conductor himself opened the door. Bill stepped back and stared. Never before had Ross shown himself when he had been there, nor even let it be known he was in.

"Why, good evening — Mr. Ross!" he stammered.

Ross didn't say anything, but he stepped back. Bill entered. Ross closed the door and led the way to the living room. Mrs. Ross, Lula, and the kid sister were there, all looking cowed and frightened. Nobody asked the newcomer to sit down or offered him a chair. He stood staring at them and fumbling with his hat.

Ross stood erect in the middle of the floor with the lips blue under the broken nose, and the hole in the head like a blazing pit. He cleared his throat and spoke in the iciest tone Bill had ever heard him use.

"I suppose you came to take my daughter to that picture show?" he asked.

"Why — er — yes, sir. I — "

"Well, you ain't goin' to do it. I've been watchin' you ever since you started sneakin' in here when I was gone an' *havin' dinner* with my wife an' children — "

"But — " the brakeman interrupted.

OLD CHARLIE stormed: "Shut up! I've not talked to you a lot, but I'm talkin' now. I've been hopin' you might take the hint that you wasn't wanted here an' stay away. But instead of that, you're comin' oftener than ever. You seem to think because I've not kicked you off my caboose, I'm gettin' soft-headed. Well, I ain't."

Silence greeted his remarks.

"An' I want you — all of you — " Ross glowered around the room, "to understand that I don't want you foolin' around my home when I'm here or when I'm not. If I ever catch you on this place again, I'm goin' to load up my double-barrel shotgun an' fill you so cock-eyed full of buckshot you'd sink in the Dead Sea. Now clear out!"

"But, Mr. Ross — "

"Don't mister me. Clear out, I said. There's no damned blanket stiff coming around here makin' love to my daughter while she sticks her feet under my table. Get out, an' don't come back!"

Kiamichi Bill got out. He did not intend to stay out. He did not intend to be bluffed, but a day or two later Mrs. Ross came to his room. She was feeling miserable.

"I'm terribly sorry about what happened that night, Mr. Burns," she said. "So is Lula. But right now there is nothing we can do about it."

Bill replied: "I'm not going to let him bluff and bully me, Mrs. Ross."

"Yes, you are. You'll have to for my sake and Lula's. Mr. Ross has acted a bit queerly since he was hurt in that — in that wreck fifteen years ago. Since that night at Dripping Springs, his condition has changed terribly for the worse. Something happened there that night — something he has not discussed with me nor anyone else insofar as I know."

Bill did not tell her about his conference behind the tie pile with Blackie Burns.

She continued: "Whatever it was, it must have upset him terribly. He's been acting like a wild man ever since. When Lula or I cross him, he goes into a tantrum, and we can't do a thing with him. Perhaps something will happen someday to clear up this unfair situation."

IV

Blackie Burns' Last Fight

BILL kept on working. He and Lula met occasionally by chance, but never by clandestine appointment. Whether it was fear, or respect, or her mother's influence, the young brake-man never knew. However, the redheaded girl did not suggest a secret tryst, neither did he. In compliance with the request of Mrs. Ross, Bill kept strictly away from the house.

Between him and Ross was never a reference to the scene that night in the living room. In fact, they seldom spoke throughout the whole summer. Ross would bring in the orders, and hand them to him with scarcely a word of comment. Bill would hang them on their hook between the cupola windows and climb into the doghouse to watch his train.

Then Ross would work at the table until the reports were done. When he had finished, he would slump in the other window, an arm's length away, and sit there staring out over the tops of the cars reeling on through light or darkness.

Kiamichi Bill wondered what passions — what hates, what fears, what jealousies — burned within that mutilated soul. He wondered where himself and Blackie fitted into the picture.

Often when the train was running and the shadow of a bum would loom dark against the firebox glow, or a head would show around the end of a box car, Old Charlie would growl like a wild thing, seize the club from under his cushion and tear out over the reeling tops to kick off some poor hobo.

Cold chills used to crawl up Bill's spine when he thought of poor old Blackie Burns, maybe out there in one of those cars, maybe coming within the range of the conductor's frenzy and having to leap for life with that old mangled body of his.

When Bill thought of that, instead of wishing the blanket stiff might come to look him up, as the old-timer had promised, he came to pray that never again might Blackie pass this way.

But Fate, working through human will, caprice and fancy, marshals the destiny of souls.

TOWARD the end of summer men were streaming eastward from the harvest fields. Always these hands had been liberal contributors to the incidentals of hustling trainmen. Although strictly forbidden by rule, it was the custom of brakemen to go over the train, collect a dollar a division, and find a nice comfortable empty where the returning harvest hand might sleep without fear of being thrown out on his ear.

That year, however, they were riding; but they were not paying; and men who tried to collect never said much about what had happened.

Kiamichi Bill did not molest them. He never did. He had not forgotten his own days on the hobo trail. He shut his eyes when he passed them and left it up to the conductor to let them ride or put them off.

It was the latter part of August when Ross had his first brush with them. They were pulling out of the Springvale yard. Four men caught a coal car six ahead of the caboose. The conductor grabbed his club and went through the side window. He strode the cars and leaped the couplings; and Kiamichi Bill saw him disappear.

For a long time he saw nothing, but as he was getting up to go find out what had happened, four men tumbled off the car into the weeds. The caboose came on. One of them picked up a rock as big as a goose egg and hurled it at the cupola. Another, a huge fellow with thick neck, and hairy chest and arms shook a fist at the brakeman and roared:

"I'll get you birds for this. I'll kill that old devil for this and you, too, you laughing hyena. I'll show you!"

He was still cursing and raving when the rattle of bumpers and clack of wheels drowned out his bellow.

When Ross returned, he had a black eye. There was a knife cut in his jumper. There was blood and hair on the brake club. Naturally Bill asked no questions and Ross gave no information.

The brakeman did not think much about it until King Lawson called him into the office. It was the first time he and the super had talked since Ross had come on the car.

"How're you and Charlie making it?" he asked.

"Oh, so-so," was the reply. "No danger our getting fired for talking too much."

Lawson chuckled, then grew serious.

"I don't want to scare you, boy," he said, "but I figure you fellows are in trouble up to your necks."

"How so?"

"Did you see that bunch of 'boes he kicked off the train night before last pulling out of here?"

"Yes, sir. I saw them down in the weeds as I came by. And were they talking! They sure were hostile."

"Know what they are?"

"Looked like a bunch of hard-boiled bums."

"Worse than that. They're an outfit that's been raising Cain in the West; and from what I've heard, they're organized and out for blood. I've warned Old Charlie; and I'm warning you. You'd better get a gat and stick it in your pants."

Bill replied: "I wouldn't know how to use it, Mr. Lawson."

He thought the super was unduly alarmed, but he bought a thirty-eight and stuck it in his pocket. Ross saw him, snorted and sneered.

BILL kept the gun a week. It was terribly in his way climbing over trains and packing hot boxes and chaining up cars. He put it into his grip a couple of runs and finally, despite official warning, left it at home.

Ross heeded the warning even less than he. Instead of staying inside the caboose with his blinds down, and letting bums ride where they pleased, Old Charlie dashed out when one showed his head and kicked him off.

Weeks passed. The incident had become an unpleasant memory to Kiamichi Bill. Then toward the middle of October, he was called for a drag west out of Oldberg.

Stars slept under the black blanket. Switch lamps loomed like colored headlights. Weird shadows moved in dark aisles between invisible lines of freight cars.

Bill hung the markers, locked the door, and started forward to couple the train line, let off brakes, and close car doors.

The first nine were empty reefers. The next was a furniture car, the eleventh was a low box, and the twelfth another furniture. He remembered it distinctly because the brake was on and the door was open.

He let off the brake, climbed down, and looked inside. A foot of old straw was over the bottom, but it was unoccupied so far as he could see. He closed the door, went to the head end, and turned back.

When he was halfway to the rear, he knew someone was moving between him and his marker. He was not frightened, because trainmen are used to seeing prowlers in freight yards.

When he was passing the furniture car, he saw the door which he had closed a few minutes ago standing open. He thought of Blackie Burns, because Blackie always opened doors of cars he intended to ride. Funny if Blackie …

He looked within. The car was still unoccupied. He closed it. Then he looked through the car ahead. It was a flat-bottomed coal car with a single crate of mine machinery blocked in its center.

It, too, held no passengers.

When he started into the way car, he quit thinking of Blackie Burns and thought of something else. The door was open. Bill had closed it before leaving. He was sure of that, but it was open now.

He looked about, but insofar as he could see nothing had been molested. He did not look in the cupola then, but when he did — when Ross had given him the orders and he was going high to read them — he came alive to the fact that the trouble train was on the iron.

Squarely in the middle of his cushion was a chunk of coal as big as his fist. Under it was a scrap of white, a corner torn from an old newspaper. He shoved off the coal and picked up the paper. On it was a scrawled message. He held it to his lantern and spelled the scrawl.

> lok out for truble. i don't no what it is. They ame to
> gang you.

There was no signature, but as Bill kept looking at it his heart skipped a beat. Although he was no handwriting expert, he thought he recognized that scrawl.

He stumbled out of the cupola. The conductor glowered up at him.

"Well!"

"I found this on the cushion. "Bill tried to control the quiver in his voice.

Ross read the warning and shoved it back. "Some crank," he grunted, "or some kid tryin' to scare us."

"In a pig's eye!" Bill retorted. "That note's from Blackie Burns."

"What!" The conductor stood up and the hole in his head became again a blazing pit. He studied the scrawl while the wheels clacked off a mile.

"You'd better get up there and watch your train," he said hoarsely.

BILL returned to read his orders. Ross made his reports and came to sit across the cupola staring silently over the tops of cars where October's rain was gently falling and freezing as it fell.

At Shanks, thirty miles out, they took water. Ross did not leave the cupola. He seldom did.

Kiamichi Bill, wishing he had heeded Lawson's warning, took the club. It was drizzling, and the earth was in utter darkness save for one green switch lamp, and the distant glow at the engine a half-mile away.

Accustomed to night and solitude, Bill had never before noticed the darkness flitting just beyond the range of his lantern's rays. He noticed it now, and to his tensed nerves it was filled with deadly' menace, with shadows, creeping, closing in upon him.

Nearing the furniture car, he thought he heard voices. He paused to listen. He heard no voices.

"Wind — " he muttered. "Wind and the rain on the roofs."

Again the door of that car was open. Again he expected it to be. Again he remembered that Blackie Burns always left doors open when he rode the empties. He looked within, but Blackie Burns was not there, nor any other living soul — only darkness and shadows and old straw and reeking odors.

He met the head man coming back.

"How're they running?" he queried.

"Like they was greased."

The boys had been guying him unmercifully about desperate characters ever since he had bought the gun. Last night he had laughed with the pal, but tonight there was nothing to laugh at.

The engineer whistled off. The pal ran for the engine. Bill waited for the rear. He stood between train and house track watching the green marker. Almost he expected a shot or a stab or a blow from the dark. It was as if Death himself were hovering around. But there was no stab — no shot.

The caboose was five cars away. Bill remembered suddenly that Ross had been alone back there in the way car. Men could have come and struck and gone in his absence. He almost feared to look within; but when he opened the door, the conductor was sitting as he had been when Bill left.

They were running ten miles an hour up Borden Hill when the shadow came. The ex-hobo saw it first, looming against the firebox glow when the tallowpot opened the door.

It showed for a moment and disappeared when the door was closed. He saw it again and again, coming closer, closer along the running boards.

It was maybe four cars away when Charlie saw it. He straightened and peered through the front window. He looked at his watch, and cleared his throat, but he didn't say a word.

THEY both watched. Like a mother quail leading the hunter away from her brood, a man — a big man — kept advancing and going back, advancing and going back.

He kept it up for ten minutes, and finally he came to the car ahead of them. He was a huge fellow wearing a sweater pulled to the ears. He must have stood there not thirty feet away while they ran a half-mile; but when they had topped the hill and begun picking up speed, he turned and went slowly forward.

Charlie brought in his lantern, and turned a hard face toward the brake-man. "Have you still got that gun?" he queried.

"Nope. A brakeman — "

"I don't need it anyhow."

He was getting up and buttoning his jumper. Kiamichi Bill had rarely offered him a word of advice; but tonight there was an inner urge, a pair of big hazel eyes looking reproachfully into his and asking: "Are you going to see him go without a protest?"

"You'd better not go out there tonight, Mr. Ross," he said.

"They can't come up here and dare me to walk the top of my own train," Old Charlie blazed.

"They're trying to toll you out so they can kill you. Stop the train at Borden, and we'll hunt them out and kick them off."

"They'll only come again. I'm going to have it out with 'em."

"Then I'm going with you."

"You can't do it. That Directors' Special will be along in twenty minutes with all the private cars on the railroad. You've got to stay and flag."

Ross was buttoning the last button on his jumper and reaching for the club.

"I tell you you'd better not go," Bill urged. "Blackie Burns — "

"To hell with Blackie Burns! He's behind the whole thing."

The old conductor went through the window into the cold rain pelting his bare, bald pate. He leaped from the caboose and charged along reefer tops, swaying now with their increasing speed.

What fear, what hate drove him on, Kiamichi Bill did not know. He did know for certain that Blackie Burns was no killer. Blackie would not harm a flea. No matter what may have been between them in other years, Blackie had been trying to give a warning of deadly peril.

Bill knew that, and he realized from the whispering voice within that, barring a miracle, the conductor had gone for the last time through the side window of this way car.

HE was an unlovely human, Charlie Ross was — cold, hard, repulsive. Certainly his treatment of Kiamichi Bill had not been such as to merit respect, friendship, or protection. Still he was human — and he was Lula's father.

Bill was a brakeman now, but no hero. The hand which pulled the lantern off the nail was trembling until he could scarcely hold it. He went below and brought a brake club from the locker — a long, heavy, hickory club.

The engineer whistled for Borden and whistled through. Bill did not swing a highball. The engineer could not have seen it on the curve. He jerked open the window and went out.

The youth paused atop the first reefer. He remembered that the special was twenty minutes behind them. If he pulled the air and stopped his train on the main line, it might hit them. If he did not, there would be no one to close the switch when they took siding at Cowled. Then the special would surely hit them on the curve.

The engine was past the switch and on the straight track through Borden. Bill darted back into the caboose, caught off a seat cushion and flung it into the track. The engineer on the special

would see it and slow.

He flung off a fusee, though he knew it would burn out long before the train came down. He waited a moment to be sure the caboose would be in sight on the straight away, and opened the conductor's valve.

The engineer whistled "broke in two." That would bring back the head brakeman. The train slowed rapidly. Bill ran the tops like a squirrel in a tree. When he had covered five reefers, the train had stopped.

He went over the first furniture car, crossed the low box and took the big one with a running jump.

Bill had as yet seen no one; but when he topped the high car, he knew a red fusee was burning in the low one ahead, and hoarse voices were cursing.

He dropped the lantern, advanced warily, and peered down. The crimson light of the fusee flickered over the scene. The rear end of the coal car was full of men.

Clubs and knives were flashing. That much he gathered from his first swift glance. At the second, he knew that a man was stretched on the floor beyond the battle, a one-armed man, and that Charlie Ross was hemmed in a corner, fighting for life.

The club swung viciously, but the odds were great. Turmoil increased. There were cries of "Let me at him!" and "I'll stick the knife in his gizzard. Thinks he's hard, does he? Well soften him!"

BILL measured his chances. The men were in a madly crowding huddle. He held tight the club and leaped into their midst. Feet struck flesh. Men went down. Some did not get up. Startled voices shouted:

"De bulls! It's de bulls!"

The conductor's club didn't miss a lick. It swung with renewed hope. Two of the gang fled from its battering blows and escaped into darkness. Four others renewed the fight.

A boot caught Kiamichi Bill while he was down. A knife was raised to strike. Before it could fall, the conductor's club stretched the would-be assassin on the littered floor.

Bill staggered to his feet. He shook his head to stop the falling stars. The fight raged on — two men battling for life, four for vengeance. Steel stung Bill's back. He whirled and struck, and the odds were three to two.

Staggering back, he leaned for an instant against the machinery crate. The three had ganged on Ross. Holding two at bay in front, the veteran conductor was backing into his corner, whence he had emerged to give help to Bill.

The bull-necked giant was there before him, waiting with an opened jack-knife. Ross did not see him. Bill did not see him. But suddenly there came a voice from the darkness, a weary, gurgling voice crying:

"Behind you, Charlie! Look!"

Bill looked and shut his eyes. Charlie looked and struck. The knife fell from a broken hand.

Bill was again in the fight, but his head was reeling. He knew clubs were raising knots, and knives were drawing blood. The head man came over the side armed with a crowbar from the section took shed.

The big man dangling a broken arm jumped; the others followed. Bill's knees buckled and he sat down against the end of the crate ....

THE birds quit singing. Kiamichi Bill opened his eyes to stare. He was in his own caboose. Charlie Ross, King Lawson, and the local doctor were working at the bunk across the aisle.

He sat up and rubbed the knots on his bruised and throbbing head. Then he staggered to his feet to look over the doctor's shoulder. A blanket stiff was on the bunk — a blanket stiff with only one arm and a grizzled beard not too clean.

Charlie Ross was holding the hand and stroking it like a woman and muttering thickly: " Take it easy, Blackie. We'll soon be through."

The doctor was bandaging the gash below the ribs in which he had taken many stitches.

Blackie was whispering: "It's no use, Doc. Le' me rest. It's all right anyhow — an' it's best."

The doctor finished with Blackie, touched Bill's bruises, and bandaged the cut under the shoulder blade.

"Kid'll be all right," he assured. "Let me know about him,"

and jerked a dubious head toward the other bunk.

The special pulled alongside and the conductor came in.

" You go on," Lawson instructed. "I'll stay here tonight. I'll ride Number Five up in the morning."

The special left town. The freight pulled over into siding and didn't go. The old blanket stiff breathed with a gurgle and a pink froth was on his lips.

" — tried to warn you — " he whispered to Kiamichi Bill.

"Yeah," Ross explained, "an' he did warn me. The whole bunch of them dirty devils — eight of 'em — was hid behind the crate in that coal car."

"I'd like to know what the devil you were doing down there?" Lawson demanded.

The conductor shrugged. "*Quien sabe?* Crazy, I reckon. Been crazy for fifteen years."

"I believe it," the super agreed.

Ross glowered at him.

"Well, anyhow, Blackie got hep somethin' was wrong an' left the note. They saw him comin' out of the caboose, an' rode her down him, never let him out of their sight after that. When I hit the floor, he yelled 'Look out!' That's when the dirty devils knifed him an' turned on me."

"I — felt like — like a' kinder owed it to yuh, Charlie," the old blanket stiff murmured apologetically.

He coughed and the froth on the lips grew redder. After a long time,' he signed for the conductor to come closer.

"You better tell 'em, Charlie," he said painfully. "The kid — ought to know."

He smiled up at Kiamichi Bill. Ross went to the rear platform and came back.

"Fellows," he said, " I want to pledge you to secrecy in this. It's best that — that some folks should never know. Right, Blackie!" He merely stated the question.

Blackie Burns nodded a little and whispered: "Right, Charlie."

THE conductor, in short terse sentences, told how twenty-odd years ago two railroad buddies had loved a woman; how Blackie McCallam — dashing, handsome, reckless young daredevil — had won; but how liquor and gossiping tongues sent an erring husband on the boomer trail, leaving a wife and child without support.

He went on to tell how the grieving wife had sent the unloved suitor out on the trail; how the suitor had found the husband "brakin' here on the S. & S."; how they had fought, and had been called, the one to flag on 1st No. 36, the other to brake ahead on the second one.

"The rest of it," he continued, " Blackie told me that night behind the tie pile at Dripping Springs. First Number Thirty-six had been carrying a boomer switchman — nearly every freight carried its boomer in those days. They had been drinking, Blackie, the boomer and the conductor, and all were pretty well lit.

"Blackie finally remembered second Thirty-six and started flagging. When he was two car lengths back, we came out of the cut. Of course, we couldn't stop. He got out of the way and let 'em hit.

"The crash sobered him. He figured he'd be sent up for manslaughter, and began figuring a way out. He always was good at figuring, Blackie was. He remembered the boomer who had been riding. They were not far from the same size. He crawled into the wrecked caboose, found the body, saw it was mangled beyond recognition, planted his watch and papers, so his wife could get the insurance, and left for parts unknown."

Ross was talking, and everybody within earshot was listening closely.

"When I came to, weeks later, I was never quite satisfied. I had a hunch Blackie had not been killed. I had seen the flare of his fusee, and had — as I joined the birds — seen him out of the tail of my eye hitting for the right-of-way fence.

"I figured it was Blackie; and I never could quite figure how he got back into the caboose. But the body had been identified; and I had no reason to doubt the identification.

"I kept in touch with Dora — that was the woman. At the end of two years, I went back to Ohio and brought her and Lula to Springvale. We did not explain; and when folks guessed we had been separated and come back together, we refused to enlighten them.

"Dora never talked about it, but I could tell from the way she acted that she had a hunch the body she could not see was not him." Old Charlie jerked a thumb toward Blackie. "Acted like she expected him to show up some day; and it made me jealous and bitter.

"Then when he showed up down here at Dripping Springs, I was ready to murder him, ready to murder this kid here because I was afraid he might spill something to Dora that would arouse her suspicions, and maybe break up my home."

"But this arm of his?" Superintendent Lawson asked. "How — "

"Another smash a year later down in Arizona," said the conductor. "Hobo smash."

Lawson said:" Well, I'll be damned! Fate's a funny thing."

KIAMICHI BILL looked at Ross. "Then Lula's not your daughter, but — "

"Mine," Blackie whispered proudly." Mine!"

The conductor nodded. The rain on the tin roof was louder and the wind was moaning softly among the pines out on the hillside. But the old blanket stiff was not hearing it, for the soul had gone beyond the sunset.

Neither Ross nor Bill talked too much when they went up the walk together two days later. The women already knew, of course, that there had been a fight, and that except for the despised brakeman, the conductor would not have been walking anywhere. Maybe Mrs. Ross accepted the explanation about a poor old bum who had also joined the fight and had been buried in the woods lot at Borden. Certainly Lula accepted it, and was happy — and that was enough for Kiamichi Bill.

Kiamichi Bill's story
continues in "Rawhider"

Rawhider

I

Cracking the Books

A LOT of folks have got the idea that any dub can be a freight conductor; but "Kiamichi Bill" Burns knew better. Kiamichi Bill knew that, with reports to be written, printed instructions to be mastered, and train orders to be read and obeyed, the job was one which required clear thought, quick decision, and a certain amount of education.

In the last respect Bill realized he was short. Only recently he had been wandering on the hobo trail; and when King Lawson, a division superintendent of the S. & S., had started him braking on the railroad Bill could scarcely read or write.

Aware that lack of education could bar him from conductor's rights, the former blanket stiff used his spare time in study. It was an uphill drag. There were no night schools in the town where he lived, no private tutors, no friends to whom he would go. A year before he was to be called up for examination Bill appealed to Mr. Lawson.

The friendly official steered him into the book-of-rules meetings for his technical training, and diplomatically arranged for

Miss Lula Ross—who was pledged to become Mrs. Burns as soon as Bill had won a promotion—to act as instructor in the three R's. Under her tutelage, the young brakeman progressed rapidly, and if it had not been for "The Duke," he would doubtless have gone into his tests, passed with the rest of the boys, and been set up running in his turn.

If it had not been for The Duke this story would never have been written, for he became part of the warp and woof which Fate was weaving for Bill and his sweetheart.

Usually Bill went to the Ross home for his lessons, but sometimes he and Lula would meet in the caboose down on its track at the foot of the stairs leading to the viaduct. As luck would have it, they were there the evening The Duke came. Under the girl's direction Bill was filling out a wheel report from an old trainbook of her father's, and footing the tonnage.

At 4.20 the caller came to announce he was getting an oil train up east at 6.00 P.M. Old Charlie, regular conductor of the crew, had been held for passenger service, and Kiamichi knew there would be an extra man on the car.

"Who are you giving us, kid?" he inquired.

Brakemen on freight like to learn beforehand who is to be their captain.

"Guy by the name of Wellington," the caller answered.

Bill thought a second.

"Wellington! I don't know—"

"New guy here. Just blew in from a new branch line down in the swamps and hired out running a train."

"Did, eh?" Brakemen almost ready for advancement resent the hiring of conductors ahead of them. "What's wrong? None of the boys up for promotion? Or is this guy some marvel brought in to show us home guards how to do it?"

The caller shrugged. "I ain't the trainmaster, brakie. But I'll say this much for him"—grinning at the girl— "If I had a sweetie like *Lula* I'd either lock her up in a pun'kin shell or else put blinders on her while he's around."

The boy laughed, and Lula threw a wad of paper at him as he dodged out the door going to call the rest of the crew.

Bill did not worry about the call boy's breezy warning—*then.* He finished his report. Teacher inspected it and called it good.

He smiled proudly, wadded the report and tossed it into the coal hod. Then, aware that Old Charlie Ross would be off the car for several weeks, they cleaned out his locker so the new conductor could use it.

They had finished and were standing very close together in the narrow opening when the caboose door snapped open, and a quick step was in the aisle behind them.

They did not require the "big hook" to untangle them. Instinct warned that the newcomer was Mr. Wellington. Lula touched crimson cheeks with a powder puff, and ran a hand through rumpled brown curls. Bill stared brazenly.

The intruder had stopped in unfeigned surprise. His handsome face was hard and his lip was curled in a smile of disdain.

"Since when," he demanded in the stern voice of one who feels the weight of new authority, "have the rules of this company been amended to permit entertaining lady friends on *our* cabooses?"

THAT little speech, particularly the way he stressed the "our," should have warned Bill this was no ordinary freight conductor. It didn't, however.

He had no inkling that the new captain was a scion of railroad aristocracy sent down to learn the game; nor that, within the year, Mr. Wellington would be telling brakemen whether they could become conductors or go on swinging a light for the rest of their days.

Bill did not like the fellow, his handsome face, nor his impudent speech and manner; but before he could say so, quick-witted Lula took charge of the situation.

"You see, sir, I'm Conductor Ross's daughter. This is my father's locker. Mr. Burns and I were just cleaning out his dirty duds."

Bill noted the quick change of expression from hostility to open admiration. All men admired Lula; the Duke was no exception.

"Your pardon, Miss Ross," he said. "Go right ahead with your cleaning; and so long as I am conductor you are welcome to come here."

While he was introducing himself as "Duke Wellington" and building up a front with the girl, Bill was bundling the "dirty duds." The Duke gallantly escorted Lula to the head of the stairs leading to the viaduct.

When he returned, Bill was cleaning and hanging markers. He looked up to see the smirk and the smile.

"Friend of yours, Burns?" There was condescension in the smooth voice.

"You mean Miss Ross?" The former hobo didn't go for condescending people.

"I didn't mean one of these!" The new man swept a contemptuous hand around the gallery of actress photos with which Old Charlie and Kiamichi Bill had adorned their palace.

Flipping color glasses in the marker to make sure they worked, the brakeman answered: "Yes, I reckon so."

"I think," said The Duke, "she's going to be a friend of *mine*, too."

He fished a cigarette from a silver case, thrust it between his lips, and smiled down upon the brakeman squatting on the caboose floor.

Battles have been fought and empires wrecked on account of women like Lula Ross; and Bill, accustomed to fighting for what he wanted, sensed that a long-drawn-out conflict was impending.

THEY left Springvale in the dripping twilight with forty tanks of casing-head gasoline. The fall rush was on. Opposing streams of traffic were dodging through passing tracks, and trains were chasing each other down the single iron.

Kiamichi Bill was soon aware that wherever The Duke had picked up his railroading, he had not learned much of it. Wellington could write reports and read orders, but he had no conception of the finer points of train operation. Bill took it for granted the man had been made on a jerkwater pike, and held himself ready to give advice when it would help move traffic.

Before the night was gray, the new skipper made it plain that he did not wish advice, especially from his brakemen and engine crew. He started it before they were out of the yards. Bill was at the head end when he brought the sheaf of orders thick enough to choke a bull. He gave one set to "Baldy" Elkins, the engineer who was pulling him, and stuffed the other into the pocket of a striped jumper.

All train and engine men are familiar with Rule 211 concerning the handling of orders, which says in part:

Copy for engineman must be delivered to him personally by the conductor, to whom the engineman will read the order aloud, and it must be understood before acted upon ...

Baldy checked the orders against the clearance and started reading them to himself.

The Duke said: "Wait a minute, there. Read those orders aloud." He spoke like a man of authority.

Baldy Elkins was a big, gruff-voiced hogger who had been pulling trains over the S. & S. for twenty years. He laughed shortly and said: "Hell, kid! I was readin' train orders when your ma was feedin' you rout of a bottle,"

"You don't seem to have read your rulebook," Wellington cut in.

"I don't need to. I know it by heart."

"Then live up to it."

The old runner grunted.

"Bushwah! I haven't read an order to a conductor since the 1903 flood."

"You'll read these to me," said the Duke. "Go ahead!"

Maybe Baldy had a suspicion this new man was not the boomer conductor he claimed to be. Baldy read his orders according to rule. When the had finished The Duke summarized them for him.

"We'll hold main line and meet Extra 1264 at Westport. Take siding and let First Number Six by us at Danville. Go to Allenby for Number One..."

Double-checking train-orders is good railroading. Usually Baldy had no objection to that, but he didn't like this young smart alec. He said scoffingly:

"Maybe, if the engine steams, an' the train runs, an' there's no hot boxes, an' Number Six is on-time."

The Duke flushed and walked toward the caboose. Bill let the train run by him and caught the caboose pulling out.

IT was six miles from Springvale to Westport up a slight grade. The old flat-bottomed 1242 was rated at twenty-one hundred tons, but that was too much. *Good* conductors knew it. They let the pencil slip and stole a hundred tons so they could go to town.

The Duke did not steal a ton. Maybe he did not know how. Maybe he feared it might blot his record later. He took it *all.*

Baldy Elkins did not make a good run to Westport. The 1242 was worn out. The coal was poor and the rails were slick. He used five minutes more than redball time.

The Duke had not said a word yet, but when they rattled by the freight in siding, he was mad as a rabid coyote and getting madder. As soon as they had cleared the switch, running twenty miles an hour instead of thirty, he cut off a string of profanity, grabbed a lantern, jerked open the door and strode to the rear platform to swing a wild highball.

Baldy answered, the two prolonged blasts floating drearily back through the September rain. He did not get moving faster. Instead, when they struck the heavier grade and his drivers began slipping, he fell down to ten miles an hour.

The Duke left his reports unfinished and walked the floor. He ranted and raved and swore. That was one thing he had certainly learned well.

"I'll show that loud-mouthed hillbilly how to kill time!" he bellowed. "I'm going over there and I'm going to tell him—"

"I wouldn't go telling Baldly Elkins too much if I was you," Bill suggested.

"I'll tell what I damned please." The reply was curt. "And when I want your advice, Mr. Burns, I'll call for it."

They were slowing then for the head man to open the Danville switch. Reduced speed had put them in a tight spot. Heading in on short time ahead of a passenger train is ticklish business. The most trifling delay or miscalculation can dash two together in rear-end collision.

Bill knew if they pulled a drawbar, or an air hose split, or a wheel left the track, he would have to jump and run back to hold No. 6. That's the time when the experienced conductor stands by to help and to oversee.

The Duke did not stand by. He had something on his mind. Slicker buttoned to his chin to keep out the rain which was now falling heavily, he was tearing out to the head end to tell the engineer.

Kiamichi hesitated to make suggestions because The Duke

did not welcome them. He did say; "Aren't you going to stay back here till we get this train in the clear?"

The Duke ignored him, and hurried ahead to rawhide Baldy.

BILL did not overhear the argument, but the fireman told him about it later, down on the Big Catalpa. The Duke used strong talk for a young conductor to use to an old engineer.

Baldy did not listen all night. When The Duke threatened to turn him in for refusing to run, Baldy lost his temper. He called The Duke a lounge lizard and a lot of other things that wouldn't look good in print.

"If you want speed," he roared, "you can get it. This scrap pile wouldn't pull a sick hen off a greased pole, but she'll sure'n hell run down hill. If you got a safety belt you'd better tie yourself into the cupola with it, because when we turn down to Roaring River we're goin' to town."

That was fast track down around Roaring River—straight iron and short, steep grades where wild engineers made sixty miles an hour with freight to keep from doubling.

Baldy Elkins was one of the wild ones who had not been tamed. Bill knew that. More than once when he had been riding the smoky end and Baldy had been pulling the hot shots, he had held his breath for a mile at a stretch as they came down on the long curve by the bridge.

But Baldy had never before made such a run as he was making that night. The section foreman declared, at the investigation two days later, that he had found three rails west of Roaring River Bridge kinked so badly he had to pull them and put in new ones.

The Duke sat in his cupola with a cigarette between his lips and a sneer on his handsome face; but Kiamichi Bill knew the cigarette was not lighted, and the slim-fingered hand clutched the window frame in a grip of steel.

Bill watched the oil tanks. They rocked and reeled, and he could almost feel the caboose wheels rise up on the curves and settle back to race away. He knew if an arch-bar ever broke or a wheel flange climbed a rail, wrecked tanks would plough through streams of gasoline like the blood of Armageddon.

They fell down Roaring River hill and made the grade in safety. Baldy whistled for Allenby and whistled a meet.

It was raining still, and the men behind could not see half-way to the engine. When they were rolling down on the passing track switch, the engineer whistled again—two short blasts in answer to a signal.

The exhaust barked, the slack went out of the train, and Bill knew they were going down the main line instead of heading in.

The brakeman was worried. Second No. 6 was close behind, and No. 1 was almost due from the east. Bill knew by the way Baldy was feeling his way into Allenby that he was worried, too, lest the operator make a mistake and wink them up the main into a trap between two passenger trains.

He looked at The Duke. Even if Wellington was aware of the danger, he did not show it.

A moment later the whistle blared a loud *whu-whuooaah!* Bill relaxed. He knew the engineer had gotten the order, and the way was clear.

THEY were running plenty fast when they passed the station. The Duke did not try to catch the order hoop. He let the brakeman do it. Bill removed the tissue and read them. The first instructed No. I to wait at Gobi until the 9.20 for Extra 1242 east. The second, although it did not mention their oil train, concerned their move-ment. It instructed Second No. 6 to use westbound track Gobi to Echner.

Gobi was the entrance to a rugged hill section called the Big Catalpa. Its tracks were built on right angles and perpendiculars. For thirty-six miles the caboose on a thirty-car train was never in sight of the engine.

There were deep cuts, short tunnels, high trestles, green pools with a slimy water trickling through moss and limestone cliffs with gnarled oak and cedar growing from them. Because it had once been the scene of unnumbered railroad disasters, the line was double-tracked from Gobi to Cowles.

The track through the Big Catalpa was safe at thirty-five miles an hour. Men with freight often ran faster. Baldy had done forty-five a hundred times when he was trying to run ahead of the varnish, and each time he had gotten by with it.

Tonight, he was just sore enough at The Duke to do all he dared—and he did it! On the upgrades the old engine hogged down to five or ten; but downhill, that's when he burned up the railroad.

They were doing forty-five when they made the curve leading out to Bannam Creek bridge. Bill was watching the oil tanks shimmy and cakewalk, and wishing Baldy would slow down a little.

Suddenly the way-car quivered as if something had struck it a terrific blow. Bill recognized it as merely the air going into emergency, but he did not know what had caused it. The thought flashed through his mind that maybe they were pulling a string of oil tanks. He half expected a flash and a flame which would be the end of time for him, and braced himself to take the shock.

The Duke did not brace himself. He stood up, reached for his lantern and commenced to swear.

All the air went off the caboose gage. Baldy whistled three long blasts, the "broke in two" signal, and followed it quickly with a *whoo-whu-whu-whu!* calling out the flagman from the rear.

Bill came quickly down from the cupola, buttoning a slicker. It was not raining hard now, but a thin mist was falling and fog was on the valley. He caught up the red lantern from beside the door and went flagging.

He did not know what was following them on the eastbound iron, but he knew Second No. 6 was coming on the westbound. He had read the orders. He did not need a conductor to tell him what to do about it. A half-mile up the hill he placed the torpedoes on both tracks as a warning and started back toward his train.

Before he reached his flagging station, four long whistle blasts called him in. When he reached the caboose The Duke was there and he was mad. Bill did not ask him what about. He did ask:

"What was the trouble?"

"Knuckle slipped by," The Duke answered shortly. "That fool hog-head was running too fast."

Bill did not remind Wellington then that he had demanded speed. They climbed back to their cupola, dragged up the hill, and turned down to Catalpa Creek.

AS SOON as Baldy had the load over the hill, he stepped out once more. Soon he was running forty-five. The oil tanks were shimmying and cake-walking again, and the caboose was reeling like a drunken bum.

The Duke brought in his light to read his watch, and counted telegraph poles for a minute. His face was red, his eyes blazing.

Bill brought his light in and read his watch. They were running forty-seven miles an hour. It was 10.40 when he put it back in his pocket. He thought Second No. 6 should be close behind them. He looked back but he could see no light through the dense fog.

As he was replacing the lantern on its hook, the air went into emergency and stopped the train again. There was nothing to indicate that the cause of this stop was different from the last one, but Bill had a vision of oil tanks turned over, spilling casing-head gasoline into the tracks.

The Duke came down swearing. He blurted: "I'm going to turn that bull-headed fool in for reckless running. There's no sense his going forty-five miles an hour on these curves."

Bill was independent enough to say: "You asked for it, didn't you?" and grinned as he spoke.

The Duke snarled: "You keep out of this, Burns, or I'll be damned if I don't turn you in, too."

"What for?" Bill inquired boldly.

The brakeman already had his equipment and was going in a hurry. He did not know why, but he was uneasy. When he was fifty yards up the track, The Duke called after him:

"Hey, you!"

Bill looked around.

"Yeah! What's the matter?"

"Remember that Second Number Six is on the westbound track, and don't you stop 'em!"

Bill didn't say whether he would or not. He had not yet thought much about it, but when he heard the whistle sounding around the curve he started running; and as sodden ties flicked back beneath heavy shoes, he was thinking rapidly.

Lately he had been in "book of rules" meetings, as King Lawson had suggested. These meetings are schools of instruction which the trainmaster or assistant superintendent conducts monthly for the education of men in train and engine service. In them the official usually presents a typed list of questions on rules and train orders and their interpretations. These questions are discussed, and the men bring up their own questions.

Bill distinctly remembered one such question which read:

You leave Cowles on No. 63 with tonnage train. Air goes into emergency and stops the train. It is dark, and you do not know what has happened. No. 8 is almost due. Will you flag No. 8, or pass it?

He recalled the discussion which had taken place. Some had said "Pass it," others "Flag it." Finally, it was brought out that under the condition, since they had no way of knowing what had happened to their own train, the safe thing to do was to flag all trains even though they were running on the opposing track.

The flagman saw he had exactly that situation here, with No. 6 coming behind him. He did not think it worth while to flag Six, because he reasoned their own stop was caused by a second slip of that coupling knuckle. Those things often slip by, especially when it is raining. He recalled also, that The Duke had told him to let her go.

ABOUT the time he decided to do it, memory flashed another rule: "When in doubt, pursue the safe course."

The flagman *was* in doubt. He darted across the track and stuck one torpedo on the right rail. A second later, he had jerked the cap off a red fusee and was waving it in the face of the passenger train speeding out of the darkness.

There was the scream of whistle and screech of brakes. The train roared by, sloughing fire. Bill felt a tinge of uneasiness then, lest he had blundered. His conductor had given definite orders; and even though Bill did not think Wellington knew what he was doing, he was in charge of the train.

Aware that the flagman on Second No. 6 would stop anything from behind, he raced down to explain to the engineer. Pullmans flicked by, with the general manager's car on the rear.

Bill raced to the engine. She had gotten five cars by his caboose. The Duke was coming on the run to meet her, swinging a high-ball.

A puzzled engineer came down to the ground. The three men met at the steps.

"What's the matter?" he asked.

"Not a damned thing," The Duke roared, "only we've broke in two. I told this brakeman not to flag you. Burns, why did you do it?"

"I didn't know—"

"Don't you know enough to obey orders? I'm writing you up for this."

Bill said: "Write and be damned!"

The conductor off No. 6 was coming. Superintendent Lawson, who had been riding with the general manager's party, was with him.

"What's the matter, men?" he inquired. "Why the big hole on this load of brass hats?"

The Duke did the explaining. He said the foot engineer was running too fast and a knuckle had slipped by.

"I told this sap-head"—he indicated Kiamichi Bill—"not to flag you, to let you come on."

Lawson said: "Did you?"

"Yes, I did. Here he turned right around and pulled a red one…"

Lawson's jaw went down, but there was a twinkle in his eyes.

"Burns," he demanded sternly, "why did you disobey conductor's orders?"

"In the rulebook meeting the other day—"

Lawson interrupted with: "Oh, you've been attending rulebook meetings, have you?"

"Yes, sir," Bill was piqued by the official demeanor. He had regarded Lawson as his friend.

NOTHING more was said, then. The engineer returned to his cab and whistled in the flag. His air whistle peeped like a drowning chicken, and they started moving.

The Duke was still talking about engineers and brakemen who

refused to take conductor's orders. Kiamichi Bill did not like what he was saying. Skippers he had known might rawhide a man to his face but they were not much on carrying tales to officials. He wondered why Lawson would listen, because the big super was not the kind of man who lets new conductors tell him how to run a railroad.

While Bill was wondering who this inefficient young upstart was who had hired in here ahead of half-dozen capable brakemen, four cars were going by. No. 6 was stepping out. Lawson and the conductor were waiting to catch the open vestibule.

They did not catch it, because before it came even with them they heard the engineer answer another signal, and heard the brakes on Second No. 6 going into emergency again.

The Duke growled: "Now what the devil?"

Nobody else said anything. The engineer called out his flag. Bill went with the others toward the engine. The head brakeman off the oil train was coming out of the cab, and the engineer was with him. Both were visibly excited.

"What is it, Breezy?" Lawson inquired.

"Come have a look," the brakeman urged.

They followed. A hundred feet down the track Baldy Elkins, looking very serious, was down with his torch inspecting a car of gasoline which had started to take a walk. It had not turned over, but all eight wheels were off the iron. The left front wheel was standing on the end of a cross-tie in the westbound main, where No. 6 would have sideswiped it and mixed six thousand gallons of gasoline with a hot engine and some wrecked Pullmans full of passengers.

The engineer, who probably would have died if Kiamichi Bill had not flagged him, turned with a bitter oath to the red-faced conductor.

"Just broke in two?" he barked.

"Why—uh—I thought," Wellington blustered. "I was sure—it

was that coupler slipping—"

"Next time you stop out on the main line where you can't see what's happened," said the hugger, "you put out a flag and tell him to stop anything. It's wet-eared students like you—"

"Mr. Wellington," Lawson interrupted, "I'd advise you to get into these book of rules meetings, and learn the intimate details of train operation on main line railroads."

II

"You May Never Be Promoted!"

BALDY ELKINS was pulled out of service for sixty days for reckless running. Kiamichi Bill received a complimentary letter from the superintendent's office. He never knew what The Duke got out of it. Nobody did.

Wellington was on the Ross car often that fall. Bill knew from the way he strutted, and the deference shown by him by officials, that he was *somebody's* son. Whose, Bill did not know and did not care.

Instead of toadying to him, and currying favor against the time when The Duke came into his own, the former blanket stiff took particular pains to refer often to the affair at the Big Catalpa.

The Duke resented it bitterly, especially after he became more efficient in his work. And he learned rapidly. Bill had to give him credit for that. He was nice to Lula Ross, too. Bill did not think much of it at first, not even when Lula quit having her brakeman at the house for his lessons and, instead, began meeting him always at the caboose.

"Things are in such turmoil now," the explained, "it's better for us to meet down here."

Bill accepted her explanation, met her in the caboose, and worked like a slave on his reading, writing, and arithmetic, preparing for that conductor's examination.

In time The Duke managed to drift in during the lessons. He would start chatting with Lulu, and, she would pay more attention to him than she did to Bill's lessons. More often than not it was The Duke, instead of Bill who saw her to the head of the stairs on the viaduct.

Next thing he knew, The Duke was laying off when there was a dance in town nights; and Bill learned with a sinking heart that they were stepping out together.

The affair reached a head when Kiamichi Bill came in one evening in October and found Lula Ross and The Duke together. How long they had been there, he did not know; but he suspected from the smirk on Wellington's handsome face and the flush on hers, that they had been there longer than an engaged girl should be alone with a man like Duke Wellington.

He took her to task for it. "Don't you think this fooling around with The Duke's gone about far enough?"

"Getting jealous?" Lula asked.

"Yes, I am," said Bill frankly. "It makes me froth at the mouth to see you continually playing up to that—"

"*You* won't play up to him. Somebody in the family should. When Mr. Wellington gets to be division superintendent or general manager, you'll be needing a friend at court."

"You don't need to be it."

"Maybe I want to."

Instead of using diplomacy, Bill lost his temper and told her to keep away from The Duke. That is where young men often make a mistake with their women. No girl likes to feel that she is being bossed. At first Lula told Bill she was his fiancée, not his slave. Next day she returned his diamond and advised him to "Get somebody else to teach you your ABC's."

OF COURSE, The Duke crowed and cackled when he heard the news, even though he had a girl back East whom he intended to marry, and wanted Lula only to play with while he was "out in the sticks." The young peacock strutted around, taking her out in his roadster and showing her off at the dances in neighboring towns.

Nothing Lula could have said would have hurt Kiamichi Bill more than that crack about teaching him his ABC's. He lost all interest in the conductor's examination, and commenced playing poker and pool instead of studying for it.

But Lawson kept track of him. Lawson believed in keeping track of his men, off duty as well as on. He realized that a train or engineman who goes out from a quarrel with wife or sweetheart may cause a million-dollar wreck by trying to take his spite out on a locomotive or a string of freight cars. He soon knew it was time for a friend to speak.

The day before Thanksgiving, The Duke and his brakeman came in on merchandise. Wellington dropped off the caboose at the yard office with his reports and bills. He and Bill almost never spoke now, except when work required it.

Bill stood out on the back platform to watch the train running into the yards. Superintendent Lawson swung up beside him. Bill pulled the markers and took them inside. Lawson was looking at a big picture of Lula Ross hanging over the conductor's table. The Duke had hung it there because, as he said, "It looked a darn sight better than the cheap photos of painted actresses which Burns and Old Charlie had on the walls."

After the markers had been put away, the superintendent said: "Sit down here, kid. I want to talk to you." As Bill sat, Lawson continued: "You're falling down on the job, aren't you?"

"Has that—that dirty cuss—"

"No, he's not complained. Besides, I don't mean your work on the car. I mean your study for that conductor's examination."

Bill answered sullenly: "I don't give a damn whether I pass it or not, Mr. Lawson."

"Oh, yes, you do. Listen, kid. I know exactly what you're up against. When a man falls for the village belle, he's in for a life of exquisite torture. Misery is the price he pays for loving a beauty. I know. I've tried it."

The official eye glistened and the chin quivered, and he lighted a stogie to hide his agitation.

Bill murmured: "Did you?"

"Yes," said Lawson. "Nobody knows better than I do, that woman is the anchor which holds man in the harbor of duty. When the cable breaks, he's either got to go on the rocks, or put to sea, and outride the storm."

Bill picked at his bill cap with trembling fingers which were all clinkered now and black as they had been that day he had come in from the hobo trail to win his way on the iron road.

"I guess you're right, sir," he said at last, without looking up.

"I know I'm right," Lawson insisted, "and unless I miss my guess, you're going to have a chance to pick up this anchor of yours right shortly, and you won't need grappling hooks to do it with."

"Do you think so?" he asked hopefully.

The super nodded. "Now you get back studying for this examination. There's a class of conductors coming up for promotion around the first of the year and you'll be in it. I don't want you to fail, because if you do, you may never be promoted on this man's railroad."

A hard glint came in the official eye, but he volunteered no further information. Bill did not ask for it. He determined to find a new teacher and go back to his old schedule, working day and night for the examination which was now little more than a month away.

THAT night he went out on the stock pickup. The rest of the crew were extra men. Duke Wellington was conductor. There was a student fireman who could not boil water, a young engineer up from passenger firing and eager to make a reputation as a high-wheeling hogger, and a student brakeman who never knew what to do nor how to do it.

That combination on stock pickup is tough on the parlor man; and to make it worse, a thin snow was falling, while the cold wind was sweeping in from the east. That's the time when trouble always comes to the iron road. Theirs started with a hot box on a car of billy-goats.

Railroads do not have many hot boxes now, but they used to be the bane of the brakeman's existence. Each freight car runs on four pairs of wheels whose axles, or journals, extend out into metal boxes. Weight is carried to the wheels through an arrangement of springs and arches to rest on the brasses, or babbitted bearing caps, which fit down over the journals.

These journals are lubricated by packing the boxes with wool or cotton waste saturated in grease. When waste runs dry, or brasses wear, or speed goes up, the wheels become hot. Unless promptly attended to, they burn journals off and wreck trains.

Finding hot boxes before they cause accidents is the trainman's duty. At first he can find them by walking along the train while it is standing and feeling each separate box with the bare hand. When they get hot, they give off the odor of burning grease to drift back along the train and he can smell it through his cupola window; or better still, from the rear platform running through a cut. When they become too hot the waste catches fire and the flare shines along the speeding train. That is the hot one's last cry for help.

They left Springvale shortly after dark with twenty cars of livestock. Their instructions were to pick up other cars at points along the line.

Engineer "Whirlwind" Sheely, eager to show his prowess, whipped the train up to fifty miles an hour and kept it there.

Bill was sure that high speed and cold boxes would make trouble. He kept sniffing through the open window. When they ran through the big cut, east of Danville, he dropped down to the rear platform. Hot box scent was there, and it was strong as skunk.

He came in and rummaged, through the supply locker. When he had filled the dope bucket and the water pail, and found the packing hook and iron, he went back to the table where the Duke was working reports.

"We've got to pull the air and cool that box," he said curtly.

The conductor looked up inquiringly. He had not smelled the hot box. He asked: "Where are we?"

"Turning down the hill to Roaring River."

"We won't stop here," decisively.

"But this one's hotter'n hell. We're apt to burn a journal off, and pile up the train."

"I'm not afraid of burning off a journal in nine miles. We'll run it to Allenby We're going in the hole there for Number One."

Bill said: "We'll have to brass it."

"Brass it and earn your money," Wellington said insolently.

THE brakeman returned to the doghouse. Soon his conductor came to sit across the cupola. When they were five miles from Allenby, Bill saw the sort of flame and knew the red-hot journal had set the packing on fire.

The Duke saw it, too. If he and Kiamichi Bill had not been scrapping over Lula Ross, he would no doubt have stopped the train then and looked after it; but a jealous man never likes to admit his rival is right about anything.

He said: "Let it blaze! We're not hauling gasoline or gunpowder."

Bill watched the flare of fire through sifting snow. At every turn of the wheel he expected the journal to break off and ditch them. He breathed a sigh of relief when they pulled into the clear at Allenby.

Aware that intense heat must have long since ruined the brass, he prepared to take it out and put in another. Changing brasses in a loaded freight car is a tough job and requires a lot of equipment. Bill selected from the supply which all cabooses carry a five-by-nine, which he reasoned would fit the system stock car. This, together with the pail of water, the bucket of dope, the packing tools, the jack, bar, block and cooler can, he placed on the forward platform, running into siding.

Most conductors help carry this stuff. The Duke never did. He was paid to carry the pencil and the book. Being a ladies' man, he wore good clothes and tried to keep them clean. Tonight he walked out through the caboose and went to the office to flirt with the female op while his brakeman brassed the journal.

As soon as Bill had the wheel jacked up, he saw there was no use doing anything to it. Heat had broken the brass to bits; these bits had cut and scarred the journal, so the car could not be taken on until it had a new pair of wheels.

Bill did not shed any tears: *He* would not have to do the explaining. That would be The Duke's job. Almost happy because the enemy had again run into trouble with his smartness, he went to the office.

The Duke was flirting with the lady op. Bill had known he would be.

Bill said: "We've got to set out that car of billygoats."

"What's wrong, with them?"

"That journal's burnt till it won't run."

"Aaa-a-a, rats! I'll go look at it myself."

They went out together. The Duke inspected it, felt of the roughened surface with a packing hock and rubbed a gloved hand over it. He did not understand much about freight cars, but he knew he did not dare start out on the main line with this one, and he realized that he was to blame.

Bill asked: "What are you going to do about it?"

"I reckon we'll have to set it out," he admitted grudgingly. "I'll go tell the hoghead. You cut the air out of it. I'll line the switches and you can spot it at the chutes so the section men can unload that stock into another car."

THE ex-hobo did not crow. If he could have seen the grinning imps of Destiny hiding up behind the water tank, he would not even have chuckled as he bled off his brakes and prepared to set out the bad order. But he did not see them.

While Bill was hunting, his hot one the student buddy, who should have been helping, was taking water instead. He had no business doing it, of course. Taking water is fireman's work, not brakeman's.

Only last night, Bill had told this same verdant youth from the hills that his place was out on the train hunting trouble when they stopped. If The Duke had not interfered, the student would *not* now have been taking water.

But The Duke had interfered. Even though he had known Bill was right, he had informed both of them that it was the conductor's place to tell his men what they should do, not the hind brakeman's. That's why the hill-billy kid had taken a dislike to Kiamichi Bill and why he was taking water tonight.

The Allenby tank was one of the old wooden affairs set up on stilts with a spout leading down to the manhole in the engine tank. When this spout was not in use it was held by weights and a chain high against the wall, where it would not knock a brakeman off the top of a moving train.

The student pulled it down and emptied two thousand gallons into the tender. He should have shoved it back where he found it; but he was in a hurry, and he was wondering if that "hard-boiled

hind brakeman" was coming over to "eat him out" again tonight. He shoved it only high enough to clear him on the tank, not high enough to clear a man standing on a stock car.

The engine crew did not know what he had done, because they were trying to fish the clinkers out of a green man's fire. Wellington did not see it, because when he went under it he was trying to figure what alibi he'd give Superintendent Lawson for burning a journal off a car of billygoats with him and his brakeman on the caboose.

That's exactly what Bill was thinking also when he cut off

the car, signaled ahead, and climbed atop it to test the handbrake, as they pulled up the passing track. He was actually laughing because The Duke had gotten himself into a tight spot trying to show his authority.

"He'll learn," Bill chuckled.

But he did not learn from that incident. Bill set the handbrake which was on the rear of the car; and when he knew it was working, released it. He was stooping over, with his back toward the hanging spout as they came on fifteen miles an hour. Unaware that it was not where it should be, he raised up as they flicked by.

Bill didn't have a chance. The spout caught him at the shoulders and sent him hurtling off into the track.

After a man falls twelve feet and strikes his head against a steel rail, he does not go on setting brakes. The Duke missed him when the car stopped above the switch. He and the head brakeman went back. They found Bill in the track with blood trickling down his face and a leg doubled under him. They thought he was dying, and they loaded him into the caboose and rushed him back to Springvale.

BILL was not conscious the next day, and the doctor said he never would be. The Duke was sorry. He was a rawhider and a bully and had other mean streaks in his makeup, but he was not a killer. He blamed the accident to carelessness of the engine crew in not replacing the tank spout.

For a full week he forgot to make his report on the journal box. When finally he wrote it up, with an apology for the delay, he did not tell the truth. He said he was working reports and Brakeman Burns was watching the train, and that he did not know the box was burning. He might not have made that statement if he had had the remotest idea Kiamichi Bill would ever get up to defend himself.

That calamity jarred Lula Ross to her senses. She did not weep nor wail; but she went to the hospital every morning and stayed there with Bill as long as they would let her.

She refused to go out with The Duke or even to see him. Although she did not know the details of the accident, the girl told herself that she was to blame. With a woman's intuition, she felt that if The Duke and Kiamichi had not been fighting over her the thing never would have happened.

So Lula gave up everything to sit with Bill all day, and hold his hand, and stroke his forehead, and tell him how she loved him. The patient did not seem to hear, but when she was there, he was quiet.

When at the end of a week the victim had not died, the doctor determined to operate. Kiamichi Bill went down into the valley. Day after day he lay in a sort of stupor. He seemed to know only when Lula was there, and to react to her presence.

In time he began to pull out, and by Easter he was sitting up and talking.

III

Fighting Mad

DUKE WELLINGTON came into his own the first of the year. The vice president of the S. & S., whose son he was, pulled the wires and had him promoted to trainmaster on the Oldberg subdivision.

Superintendent Lawson knew it was a terrible mistake. He told the higher officials it would mean the ruin of the boy and make trouble among the men. He pointed out that The Duke did not know railroading from any angle; that he could not get along with men; that he was spiteful and vindictive; and that he was still sowing his wild oats to bring forth the harvest.

"Before he finds out he's not God Almighty in person," Lawson told the proud parent, "he's going to pull some bonehead that'll make you and him both wish you'd never been born."

The father glared in silence.

"Set him back braking!" Lawson urged. "Strip him of authority instead of giving him more. Just as sure as you make him trainmaster, you're highballing this pike straight into a catastrophe of some kind."

But the pompous vice president was the old block of which The Duke was a chip off. With the devil's help, he had collected a few million dollars that other men had produced, and now he was using it as a club to get what he wanted for himself and his family.

Thus The Duke became trainmaster, even though he was not qualified to be a good scissor-bill.

Right away trouble started. Except for an efficient trainmaster's clerk who handled the routine, Wellington would not have lasted a week. Even so, the brunt of the work fell on the superintendent's office. But worst of all was the human grief which came.

Theoretically the trainmaster is responsible to the superintendent for hiring, promoting, and firing train service men; and for discipline among the engine men. But discipline was not The Duke's forte, even though he *thought* it was.

To begin with, he had a host of enemies. He and Baldy Elkins had been at war ever since that first trip and Baldy, being a good engineman, had a drag with the Brotherhoods. Then, too, when Kiamichi Bill Burns was able to tell his side of the hotbox story, everybody who knew the two men realized that The Duke had deliberately lied about a dying man, and that did not raise his popularity.

By the time Bill was ready to return to work, the new trainmaster had become the most despised person who had ever sat in a swivel chair on the S. & S.; but since he could not be removed until he had brought about real trouble on the iron, young Wellington did as he pleased and got away with it.

BRAKEMEN are examined in "classes" and promoted to conductor. A class of four had been called up and promoted in December. It was then Lawson had hoped to see Burns establish his conductor's rights, but at that time Bill had been lying on his back staring up at the ceiling and trying to remember what had hit him.

When he learned that The Duke had been made trainmaster Bill was filled with apprehension. On the S. & S. there were no fixed standards of achievement which one must meet as there are in most cases of examination.

A conductor must know his book of rules, must understand all kinds of train orders, and be able to distinguish the good from the bad. He must be able to make out reports required by the company. Above all, he must prove his ability to use good judgment in case of accident or emergency.

The trainmaster, often with the advice of the superintendent, decides what men are to be called up, selects questions, conducts the examination, and determines whether the applicant is, in his judgment, qualified to be given the job of running a train.

If an applicant is rejected, he may try again within six months, or a year, after further preparation. If he does not pass within reasonable length of time, he may be advised to "pass up his conductor's rights." In that case it is up to him to find employment on another road and climb the seniority ladder, or else go on braking the rest of his days.

As soon as he was able, Kiamichi Bill went back preparing for the examination, which he knew he would be called to take in the fall. Lula helped him now with vigor such as she had not shown before.

"You've got to have everything down pat, boy," she told him. "I *know* that four-flusher. If he has a ghost of an excuse he'll turn you down."

"The Duke won't need an excuse," Bill said gloomily. "He's running this job and he knows it."

Nevertheless Bill worked hard and faithfully.

He knew the rules, knew train orders, could make reports. Even so, he was uneasy. That matter of judgment is the intangible thing. Most men are turned down on account of it than on any other ground, especially now since one is seldom hired who has not at least an elementary education.

The young brakeman was still more uneasy when, in October, he was called in with a dumb-bell who had failed four previous examinations. He was certain that the class had been arranged for his especial benefit, because he knew The Duke could save his own face and keep him out of his rights for another six months at least by turning him down in an examination in which nobody passed. However, there was nothing he could do but take it.

Bill felt bitter because he knew his injury was the direct result of The Duke's contrariness. Still, he had not mentioned it to Wellington, and the latter had always tried to look the other way when they met.

THIS morning The Duke could not look the other way. He had to face the two men across the table and ask his questions. He started in his bulldozing manner, trying to rattle them.

The dumb-bell went to pieces under the barrage of hotshot questions, but Bill kept his head. The Duke had sorted out all the tough ones he could find on record since officials had begun examining conductors. Bill answered most of them—right. Not all. No man could answer them all right.

The Duke, with the aid of a dispatcher who was a kindred soul, had gotten together as nasty a lot of trick orders as were ever put on a hook. He threw them down for his applicants to sort out. The dumb-bell mixed many of them. Bill mixed a very few.

Wellington then gave data for switch lists, wheel reports, delay sheets, and the rest, and Bill completed them without an error. Then he turned back to a lot of trick questions, asking "What would you do then?" "What would you do now?" "How would you handle this situation?"

Bill thought the answers he gave displayed good judgment. Evidently The Duke did not agree. He rejected the dumb-bell and Bill also.

Superintendent Lawson seldom questioned the decision of a train-master, but he questioned that one.

"What was the matter with Burns?" he inquired searchingly.

"He'll never be a conductor!" The Duke did not look at Lawson.

"Why not? Doesn't he know his rule book and his orders?"

"Yeah. He knows 'em fairly well."

"His reports? Can't he write them?"

"After a fashion, yes."

The Duke was sullen and red behind the ears. Lawson kept asking questions.

"Then, for heaven's sake, why didn't you promote him?"

The Duke leaned over the desk, defiant as a lion at bay. He demanded:

"Are you in the habit of putting assistants through an inquisition who do their duty as they see it, sir?"

Lawson shrugged, bit the end off a cigar.

"Don't need to go getting huffed up over it, Mr. Wellington. I just wanted to know whether you *knew* why you turned Burns down."

"Of course, I know why I turned him down. I don't like the ignorant, illiterate sucker; and I don't aim to ever see him set up running a train as long as I'm trainmaster on this district."

"I don't believe I'd talk much about that reason, Mr. Wellington, if I were in your shoes. Suppose Burns should happen to hear it?"

BURNS heard it. The Duke tanked up on rotten liquor and got talking official secrets with a girl out at the night club. The girl passed the news on to Lula Ross, and Lula told her fiancé.

That was along in November, just about a year after he had been injured. Lula's father was back on the car then. They had been called for another stock train; and Kiamichi was eating six-o'clock dinner with them, when Lula told him.

Bill didn't say much. He asked in a quiet sort of voice: "Did she really tell you that?"

"She sure did!"

"Somebody ought to take that guy out and horsewhip him," Ross remarked.

The brakeman did not say what he intended doing, whether anything; but he did not eat much dinner; and his eyes were on fire when he arose from the table.

Lula usually walked down through the yards with him and her father when they went to work and came back over the viaduct. Bill went by his room for his lantern which he had left there this morning when he had come in before daylight. He hung it on his arm without lighting it.

As they came to the yard office, The Duke swung off the superintendent's private car which was pulling into its track beyond. Without paying them the least notice, he strode by and went toward the terminal building.

Bill went into the yard office to find out where his train was made, and when he came out there was a light in the trainmaster's office.

He stared at the light a long time, as if it fascinated him. Lula's father went toward the caboose. They started following him. When they had walked fifty yards, Bill stopped.

He said: "I think you'd better go back the way we came, sweetheart."

The girl was surprised.

"Why? Don't you want me to go?"

"Not tonight. After I've got a little chore to look after before I leave this burg."

Lula didn't question what that chore was. Bill escorted her out to the street, and came back into the yards. When she was at the middle of the block, she remembered how silent he had been all evening, and how he had stared at the light in the trainmaster's window.

"He surely wouldn't be fool enough—" she murmured. Then: "I couldn't blame him, if he did…"

As soon as the girl was out of sight, Bill went to the terminal building. The door into the trainmaster's office was open. He walked in and closed it and the night lock snapped.

THE Duke looked up from rummaging through his papers. Then he shoved back his chair and got to his feet. His eyes were just a little wider than usual. He said: "What is it, Burns?" He forgot to sneer that time.

Bill walked around the desk and stopped close beside him. He still had the lantern on his arm, but he did not know it. He tucked the thumbs under the straps of the overalls, and rocked gently on the balls of his feet.

"I just heard why you turned me down on that conductor's examination, Wellington," he said softly.

"Why, I turned you down because—"

The soft tone suddenly died in an explosion of pent-up wrath. "Because you didn't like that ignorant, illiterate sucker, and you don't ever intend—"

"Did Lawson tell you that?"

Bill got himself under control again. "No, you blabbed it yourself the other night when you was drunk out at the dance hall."

"You'd better take it easy, Burns," said the official. "I won't stand—"

"I've stood a devil of a lot from you, Wellington. You've been trying to rawhide me around here and bull things through ever since you've been here. You've half-killed me, and now you've refused to promote me when I know and you know I'm ready,"

"So what?"

Bill's answer was deadly. "I've come in here to beat you with my bare hands till you get down on your knees and beg for mercy."

The Duke's eyes were darting hither and yonder like those of a cornered bobcat.

"You can't do that, Burns."

"But I'm *going* to!"

"I'll fire you!" screamed the dandy. "I'll see that you—"

"You won't get a chance to fire me," came the ominous reply. "I'm resigning, right now before I start."

The Duke was trembling and he was white. He was as big as the former blanket stiff; but his muscles, sapped with dissipation and soft from disuse, were no match for the hard ones of his opponent, even though the latter was less than four months out of the hospital.

Bill ordered: "Pull off your coat! You've done a hell of a lot of talking, now you're going to do some fighting."

Bill set the lantern on the desk and began to unbutton his jumper. The Duke watched until he had one arm out of it, then dashed a hand quickly toward the drawer.

The brakeman beat him to it. As the drawer came open, and light glinted from the blue barrel of a thirty-eight revolver, he smacked the trainmaster in the face with his jumper, jerked his

arm out of the sleeve and picked up the lantern.

"Leave that gun where it is!" he ordered. "Another crooked move out of you and I'll wrap this lantern around your bull neck so tight it'll take both wreckers a week to untangle you from it."

The Duke looked toward the door, and tried to reach it. Bill blocked him.

"Quit stalling! I'll give you till I count ten to get out of that coat. *One—two—three—four—"*

WHEN Lula remembered how Kiamichi had looked at that light in the trainmaster's office, she suddenly started walking briskly back to the yards. Turning the corner, she saw Bill disappear behind the terminal office. The girl knew that if he went in there to attack Duke Wellington, he would come out a jobless man, or perhaps come out in the patrol wagon.

Lula considered following him, but realized she could not control him. She broke into, a run, heading for the yard office. As she paused at the door, the girl saw her father's light down by the viaduct. She whirled and sped toward it. Fifty yards away, she began calling:

"Dad! Oh, Dad!"

Old Charlie Ross heard her and came on the run. Superintendent Lawson, whose car was now standing on the second track over, had stopped for a word with the conductor. He, too, came running.

Ross was asking anxiously: "What's the matter? What's wrong? Where's the boy friend?"

"He's—gone—to the trainmaster's office," Lula panted. "Hurry! Quick! You've got to get to him before he does anything. If he strikes that Duke Wellington—"

Lawson did not lay claim to dignity. He sprinted, toward the office, with Old Charlie at his heels and Lula following. As they passed, two lounging switchmen joined the procession.

When they reached the door which was locked, Kiamichi Bill was counting, *"Five—"* They could hear him through the transom. *"Six—"* Lawson shook the door and called, but nobody answered. The count went on, *"Seven—"* Lawson fumbled for a pass key. *"Eight—"* The pass key went into the lock. *"Nine—"* The key turned. The door burst open.

The new arrivals stopped. Wellington, white as a ghost, was between the desk and the filing cabinet. His coat was hanging on one arm, and his eyes were as big as saucers. Kiamichi Bill was flexing his big fists and poised for the spring. Lawson grabbed him as he was leaving the floor.

Men had done a lot of things to Kiamichi Burns since he had

come to Springvale; but in all the months, no one had ever before seen him fighting mad. Tonight, he struggled and almost wept as he begged them: "Let me at him! Leave me alone! I'm going to beat him—"

They held Bill Burns until he was quiet. By that time The Duke had regained his equilibrium and started showing his authority, He blustered:

"I'm going to fire you for this, Burns. I'll fire you just as sure—"

Lawson's big jaw came down, and the stogie felt out of his mouth in two pieces.

"Listen, you," he said shortly. "You're not going to fire anybody for this. If you try it, I'll take you over my knee myself and paddle you with a board till you can't sit down for a week. You get down to business and do your work the way it ought to be done, and let these men alone when they're trying to do a job railroading."

IV

The Duke Takes a Long Shot

FOLKS in the know figured the trouble was not done on the Oldberg sub. They reckoned that by the time The Duke relayed his version of the affair in the office to the old block of which he was a chip off, there was going to be a new superintendent, and possibly a lot of new names on the seniority lists.

How it   would be brought about, they did not know, for The Duke suddenly became as wary as a wolf in the mean things he was doing; but they sensed trouble ahead.

The Duke had been riding freights ever since he had been trainmaster. That was his business, to check up on the men under his control, to see that they were doing their duty and hitting the ground with both feet.

Particularly he began checking on Ross and Burns. He had

an excuse, of course, but it seemed to them he spent most of his time riding their car; and they knew that he was not riding with them because he loved their companionship.

He was riding with them the night hell's angels got ready to gasp with horror. They had gone into Oldberg on an oil drag the night before, and were getting out at 10.40 that morning. The S. & S. had been stung by the tonnage bee and that winter had bought a lot of new engines, half million-pound decapods with stokers in the cab and boosters on the tank wheels.

Always when the big engines come to the iron, traffic is upset and schedules are shattered. Men used to handling thirty or forty car trains do not readily adjust themselves to handling double that number. They kick and howl, and officials accuse them—not always without reason—of deliberately causing delay to prove the big ones will not work successfully.

That's what was happening on the S. & S. Firemen did not know how to operate the new stokers. The purchasing department had not learned what kind of coal to buy. Sidings built to hold fifty or sixty cars would not swallow eighty or ninety, so that freights had to lose time sawing passenger trains by.

Seldom a trip but the engineer managed to pull out one weak draw-bar and sometimes a half dozen; and that, with the bad weather of the early winter, tied things up so that crews were often a week getting a single train over the road.

THAT was The Duke's alibi for riding with Ross and Burns. Either the breaks of luck or the deliberate scheming of an unfriendly trainmaster and dispatcher kept them almost constantly on the drags hauled by the big engines.

They drew one of them out of Oldberg that trip. Kiamichi Bill saw when he was letting off the brakes and getting ready to leave, that it was an eighty-car drag of mixed freight. Just about everything was in it—cars of scrap iron, steel rails, and machinery, feed and flour, tanks of acid and benzine and naphtha.

They even had a couple of cars of dynamite in the middle, but he never gave a thought to that. Men don't worry much about what kind of load they are hauling so long as it stays on the iron and doesn't run hot.

Baldy Elkins was pulling them, and though Baldy had been out of service for one offense or another half the time since The Duke had been trainmaster, he still had not learned to be a "yes-yes" man.

When Bill got over to the engine, Baldy was crabbing about eighty-car trains and engines so big a man had to have a spy glass to see past the boiler-head, and was expressing his opinion of railroad officials who didn't know how much one of them would pull nor how to run a railroad.

He was still talking when The Duke came out with Conductor Ross, bringing the orders. Baldy didn't say anything to The Duke, but asked Ross:

"Didn't they have any more cars they could tie to this iron elephant's tail? It's a damned shame to go all the way to Springvale with only four thousand tons."

The Duke said: "If you don't like the kind of trains you pull on this railroad, why don't you find another one that lines them up to suit you?"

Baldy winked at Bill and answered slyly: "I'm afraid I'd never find another trainmaster that I love like you."

The Duke got mad. He could dish it out, but he couldn't swallow it. He quickly changed the subject. In his nastiest tone he said:

"I'm telling you, Elkins, I want you to get this train over the road today. I'm riding with you fellows and I want you to make better time than you did last trip up."

Last trip up, Baldy left four draw-bars scattered along the right-of-way; the hogs had caught them at Borden; and they had been thirty-one hours hauling a train a hundred-thirty miles.

With a grin, Baldy drawled: "All right, Mr. Wellington. With you along to help and encourage us, I'm sure we'll make this trip in good shape—maybe get home in time to go to church with the wife tonight."

THEY left Oldberg running as Extra 21, with right over No. 34 to Dripping Springs, and the understanding between engineer and conductor that they would go in the hole at Farmington to meet No. 10, the St. Louis Express.

Baldy made a good run to Farmington, much better than The Duke had anticipated. When he whistled for the station, he whistled a meet. The Duke was in the cupola smoking a cigarette and staring out over the wooded hills with snow clouds thickening in the icy sky. He jerked out his watch.

"Why don't you highball him?" he asked Ross sharply. "You've got plenty of time to go to Tamerlane for Number Ten. That's the reason you fellows never get anywhere with these trains. You sit up here in the cupola and sleep instead—"

Ross did not explain that he had eighty cars, while Tamerlane held sixty-one; that if he went Tamerlane, he would have to flag Number 10 and saw them by; but that if he stayed at Farmington he could be doubling his excess cars over into the house track while the varnish was coming, and have the main line cleared when it arrived.

A smart young trainmaster who had been conductor on the district should know that much.

The old conductor merely said:

"Okay, Mr. Wellington. We'll go to Tamerlane if you insist."

"Certainly, we'll go to Tamerlane. There's no sense staying here when we've got time to go down the road."

Ross winked at Kiamichi Bill and, in the tone of voice the cat used before it swallowed the canary, told him; "All right, kid. Get out there and give that hogger a high sign."

Bill climbed atop the cupola with a newspaper. The head end could never see a hand signal three quarters of a mile. He waved and waved and finally Baldy answered.

By the time they reached Tamerlane, The Duke had no doubt come alive to the fact that they were going to meet the express at a sidetrack too short to hold their train, but didn't mention it.

They headed in and left the nineteen cars sticking out on the main line. The head brakeman flagged No. 10. That would not have caused a lot of delay, if it had not been for another upset.

THE dispatcher, knowing that Ross never moved a freight into a hole where he knew he was going to have to delay a passenger, and figuring he would stay at Farmington for the Express, had authorized No. 34's conductor to put a flag on No. 10 and go to Farmington for them.

This flagman broke the news to Baldy, but the engineer did not dare pull out into the face of No. 34 until the man had gone back around the curve to hold them. That took several minutes. When No. 34 was stopped, Baldy pulled the rest of his train in the siding and let No. 10 go. That put them out with a twenty-five-minute delay.

After the express had gone, the extra backed out so No. 34 could come up the main line. No. 34's conductor dropped off the engine, where The Duke and Charlie had now gone, and inquired:

"How many cars you fellows got?"

"Eighty's all," Ross answered. "And you?"

"Sixty-nine." The conductor grinned.

"Uh, oh!" There was triumph in Ross's voice. "I see where we make a double saw."

That double saw was what started them on the long day. Ross

had to walk three-quarters of a mile to tell Kiamichi Bill what they were going to do. He *walked;* he didn't run. He was in no particular hurry.

They cut twenty cars off clear of the switch, and Baldy pulled the rest into the passing track. No. 34 came on by, shoved the twenty ahead of the engine toward Oldberg to clear the west switch.

Baldy pulled his sixty cars two miles down the main line toward Dripping Springs. No. 34 backed down behind him, cut off the engine, shoved the twenty into the passing track, coupled up and left town. Baldy came back to get his train together.

By that time, it was 2.40. They had been here nearly three hours. The Duke, having forgotten he was responsible for the jam, was on the warpath accusing both crews of stalling, of killing time, of trying to lay out these freights to show the officials they couldn't be handled. The men let him storm and rage.

It was 2.50 when the air brakes were pumped up. No. 4 and No. 7 were due to meet there at 3.30. Since the extra lacked a few minutes time to go to Dripping Springs for No. 4, they flagged both trains, sawed them by, and laid them out nearly an hour.

Then with No. 8 coming from the west, they would probably have been there the rest of the night, if The Duke had not ordered them to put a flag on No. 5 and follow Dripping Springs. That got them out of their first jam, but it was 4.30 when they were ready to leave Dripping Springs. They had made twenty-four miles in six hours!

AT the end of the next eight hours they were pulling out of Allenby, twenty-two miles from Springvale. It was midnight. They had trains to meet. It was two hours until they'd be tied up by the hog law, and it was snowing hard now.

During those fourteen long, hard, rawhiding hours, The Duke had found no less than twelve offences for which to fire every member of the crew, including insubordination, and he was swearing by all things holy he was going to do it just as soon as ever he could get them into terminal.

They went into the hole at Roaring River to meet No. 6. Roaring River had room for them. They did not have to saw by. They made a good meet and were pulling out with time to go to Springvale for No. 32 and No. 2.

They had a student brakeman on the head end, again. Always there were students railroading during the rush winter months when railroading was at its worst. There used to be some pretty good ones when "Pop" Hollister had been trainmaster, but since The Duke had gone hiring the kind who bowed and scraped to him instead of the hard-headed fellows who stood on their own feet and fought for their rights, the crop had become pretty worthless.

This one was a nervous youth. He was scared stiff for fear he would do something to get fired for, and not strong enough to stand the gaff of sixteen-hour days rawhiding around, sawing by and doubling. He was asleep in the cab when No. 6 came through Roaring River. The fireman woke him up, and in a sort of daze he stumbled out to open the switch.

There was ice on the lock and it took him a long time to get the key into it. When he finally got the switch unlocked, Baldy was coming on dragging the eighty cars out toward the main.

That made him nervous, because he was afraid Baldy was going to split the switch and tear it all to pieces. He flicked it over, as the pilot wheels were curving toward it, and set the lock back into the hasp.

Pulling out of sidings, the head man hooks the lock back into the hasp, and leaves it unlocked so that the hind man can get it loose in a hurry. This time the student snapped the lock. The train headed out around the maze of curves where a man could not pass a signal twenty car-lengths, even in fair weather.

In a case like that, the head brakeman climbs into the cab and counts telegraph poles pulling out. Allowing three cars to a pole, he can figure pretty close to when his caboose will come through the switch. When the student counted twenty-six, Baldy eased off, allowed Kiamichi Bill time to close the switch and catch the caboose. Then he started picking up speed, making a run for the hill beyond the bridge.

The student had evidently missed his count on the poles, for they slowed down six car-lengths too soon, and the engineer had whistled off and started moving when the caboose was coming through the switch. Bill knew he was going to have to hurry, for there was a little down grade to the bridge, and the big engine yanked the train out rapidly.

He grabbed for the lock in the darkness. It didn't come out of the hasp. He didn't take time to swear about it. Instead, he snatched the switch key out of his pocket by its leather chain, and unlocked it. By that time the caboose was five or six car lengths down the line and running at rather good speed.

Kiamichi struck out chasing it. His foot slipped on a slick tie and he went down into the snow, putting out his lantern. That was hard luck. A man without a lantern can't make much speed over a railroad.

THE conductor was watching. He too had seen, when the train began picking up speed too soon, that there was need for quick work. He stepped inside, opened the brake valve and started bleeding the train line.

It's hard to pull the air on an eighty-car train without bad results. He held it open, only for a second, intending it to be a signal to the engineer to stop; but it didn't work. The brakes went into emergency. All the air went off the gage, and before Bill limped up to the caboose, the engineer was whistling his "broke in two."

The Duke had gone into the cupola. He came out swearing and spluttering. He accused Bill of falling down on purpose to hold the train, so they would have to tie up under the hog law. He accused the conductor of pulling the air so as to break the train in two, and he swore for the thirteenth time he was going to fire the whole crew just as soon as they got into Springvale.

"And you don't need go running to your friend Lawson with it, either," Wellington stormed. "It won't do any good. If that idiot interferes in my business again, he's going out too; and I'll take the job myself."

That was the boast The Duke made there at Roaring River while they were chaining up a car and having it put away; but it was the last boast he ever made to the boys on the S. & S.

The men did not need to be told what had happened. Even Wellington knew. The sudden setting of brakes on an eighty-car train with a big engine straining at the bumpers had pulled out a draw-bar. They spent an hour and ten minutes getting the crippled car put away in siding at Roaring River, so they could go on. That left them fifty minutes to go into Springvale.

That was running time. If everything went right they could make it. But there was No. 32, now due out of Springvale. They could make Danville, five miles up the hill, but they could not go on in.

The Duke rushed into the office, told the dispatcher to give them an order which would let them go in without tying up.

The dispatcher put out an order: "No. 32, Eng. 41, take siding meet Exa 21 west at Westport." Westport was halfway down the slight grade between Danville and Springvale. They left town, intending to go to Westport for No. 32, and make it in home just under the wire.

But Fate had grown tired fooling with Duke Wellington. Tonight was his night. Pulling out of Roaring River, the fireman had had his fire built up to stand a genuine beating on the run for the hill. After the train stopped and had stood for an hour and ten minutes, his fire went black with clinkers; and for the rest of the night he couldn't get it back into shape.

Halfway up the hill the hands of the clock began going backward, and they doubled into Danville.

IT WAS 2.35 when they got the train into siding at Danville. They had been working sixteen hours. The hog law had them. If they turned another wheel, the last man of them would be liable to fine and imprisonment for violation of the Hours of Service Act. The wheels stopped turning.

The fireman fixed the fire so it would neither die nor boil away all his water. The engineer shut off the air pump and the injector. Conductor Ross reported to the dispatcher that he was tying up; and the crew all went to the little restaurant uptown to fill stomachs that had not been filled since morning.

The Duke did not go for the lunch. When the crew had gone, he waded through the snow to the engine. That was one thing about The Duke; he was not lazy, especially if he thought he had a ghost of a show to find something to fire a man for. He had no intention of doing what he did, but he went into the cab and looked about.

Now, Duke Wellington understood a little of the mechanism of a locomotive. In two years braking on the branch line he had learned how to set throttle and reverse to start one, how to handle the air brake valve to stop it. While the agents had been instructing firemen in the use of the mechanical stoker, he had learned a little about that, too. He knew how to start the stoker engine and set the jets to put coal enough into the firebox.

Unaware how dangerous a little learning is, the trainmaster conceived the notion of taking this freight train into town all by himself. The crew had tied up. They had had a meet with No. 32 at Westport; there was nothing else due out of Springvale until

No. 2 and he had time to go down there for them.

Not thinking that when that crew had tied up, the dispatcher was going to cross Extra 2 out of the picture and go on running a railroad, he arranged with the pumper to open the switch for him to go out and shut for him after he had gone.

Then, without so much as a whistle to warn the men in the restaurant that he was leaving town, The Duke started easing gently down the slight grade out of Danville.

KIAMICHI BILL was the first one through eating. While the rest of the boys were sitting around the table figuring how they were going to pull a big strike on the S.& S. in case The Duke fired them without just cause, Bill decided to return to the caboose and go to bed.

The railroad was a quarter-mile from the restaurant. When he came within hearing distance, he discovered the train was moving. He could not understand it, because the regular crew was uptown, and he knew no train had come in to bring a relief crew.

Bill broke into a run, thinking the brakes had leaked off and the train was rolling out. Before he reached the track, however, he heard the gentle *whoosh-whoosh- whoosh* of the exhaust and knew there was a hand at the throttle.

He grabbed the caboose and ran in to pull the air; but when he looked at the gage the hand was down against the peg. *There was no air.* He dashed back to the platform and looked ahead. The pumper's light was at the switch. As he went by, clicking out on the main line, Bill shouted:

"Who's on that engine?"

"Trainmaster!" the pumper shouted back. "He's takin' her on into Springvale."

Bill realized right away they were going into trouble. Since they had tied up, the dispatcher could now move No. 32 out of Springvale. If that happened, with this blizzard blowing and the snow pouring down so a man could not see a hundred yards ahead of him, there was bound to be a "cornfield meet" which would make some new widows in Springvale.

Then he began seeing other possibilities. He did not know why there was no air in the caboose, but he made some guesses. He thought the engineer would have turned off the air pump before leaving the engine, and he decided The Duke would not have gumption enough to know how to cut it in.

If Wellington didn't, he would go right down the main line in Springvale, intending to make a grandstand stop, turn an empty brake valve, and then keep right on going through town.

There would be switch engines in the way, maybe a passenger train, maybe a string of freight cars. The big hog with eighty cars trailing it would go plowing right through them. Bill almost smiled when he pictured the look of blank astonishment which was coming over The Duke's handsome countenance when he shoved the brake valve and the train didn't stop.

"Maybe that'll take the starch out of him," Bill muttered. "Nothing else ever has."

Then he remembered some of the things which those eighty cars carried—scrap iron, benzine, naphtha, dynamite, maybe tanks of sulphuric acid. It would not be a nice train to ditch in a busy terminal. If that naphtha caught fire, for instance; or if the dynamite exploded ...

HIS first impulse was to start setting hand brakes; but he knew The Duke would go working steam against him, and the brakes would not do any good. He figured his best chance was to go over the tops, try to reach the engine as soon as possible, and cut in the air pump to raise pressure before they went down into Springvale.

He hit the tops running They were slick with snow, but the former blanket stiff was used to that. He had no time to be careful.

While he was running three quarters of a mile over them The Duke would be putting miles behind him. They might not make it. They might plow head on into No. 32 in the blinding snow and blow the whole outfit into kingdom come. Bill didn't take time to think about that.

Slipping on the snowy tops which were now reeling gently at thirty miles an hour, he raced on, leaping blindly down into coal cars where objects buried in the snow might break a leg or knock him senseless.

They were running through Westport when Kiamichi Bill stumbled through the coal gate and fell into the gangway. The Duke looked around with a smirk and said:

"Well, where did you come from?"

Bill shouted: "Your air pump! Cut in your air pump!"

"Air pump!" Complacency gave place to mild concern.

"Yes, your air pump!" Bill repeated. "You've not got a squirt of air in your trainline. You're going to plow right into Number Thirty-two somewhere down here. If you don't hit, you're going down into Springvale in the face of passenger trains without a sign of a brake on this outfit. You—"

The Duke was hunting for the valve which cuts in the air pump. He did not know which one it was. Bill shoved him out of the way.

Bill cut in the pump. It started racing madly. Air pressure was soon climbing, but eighty cars is a long drag. It would take minutes

to get enough air into those cars.

The brakeman soon had the whistle going. He had the reverse hooked up and the throttle closed. He expected every moment to see the headlight of No, 32 dart into his face, and feel the impact of a head-on collision, but there was nothing he could do.

He knew be must have at least sixty pounds of air showing on his gage before he dared use it. He *should* have seventy, but with the slight grade he might get by with sixty. He would not dare try it with a pound less.

When he whistled for the milepost, he had more than fifty. He was standing up on his platform. The Duke was slumped in the fireman's seat. Both of them were staring dead ahead with sweat bursting out from cold faces.

IN Springvale the dispatcher was busy. He had two sections of No. 2. The first—the regular equipment, twelve standard Pullmans—would pull up the main line at 3.30. The second— private cars of officials going to a traffic conference—would pull up No. 2 main line, ten minutes later. Both would be there twenty-five minutes changing engines.

As soon as he learned Ross had tied up at Danville, he began planning to move No. 32 out of town, just as Kiamichi Bill had expected. Shortly after The Duke had pulled by the switch, he got hold of the conductor, annulled the meet with the extra, and told him:

"Now get going just as soon as you can. I want you to go to Westport ahead of these passenger trains. Don't try to go to Danville, because Danville's full."

They did not get going right away. The conductor had to walk half a mile to the engine. He took his time. There was no use running.

The engineer read the order. Reading orders is a particular job. He did not question this one. He called out the head brakeman to open the switch for him and got the train in motion.

The brakeman waited at the switch. The engine came toward him. The pilot was curving out on the main line.

He turned to catch the engine step, but before he caught it, he heard a sound breaking in above the crash of the exhaust. He tensed, and listened.

There was no mistaking it. A locomotive was whistling for the milepost, and she kept whistling. He knew by the sound she was one of the big decapods, and she was not standing still.

He let out a war whoop, dashed for the engine step, swung a "stop" sign and changed it to a "back up." The engineer used his air. He thought they were on the ground.

He called: "Whatsa matter now?"

"Get back in there, quick! That extra! It's coming down here like hell!"

The engineer doubted this, but did not take time to argue. He set his reverse in backward motion, and started toward the yard office.

The brakeman dashed to the switch. By the time he had it closed, the extra was right on top of him whistling a terrified warning, and he was swinging a stop sign.

KIAMICHI BILL thought he was going to sideswipe No. 32. He held his breath for five endless seconds, expecting the two pilot bars to lock, expecting his engine to go flipping over on its side or to turn crosswise of the track with freight cars spilling over. Five seconds, and then he knew he was safe by No. 32.

Bill had already used what air he had. It was slowing the train down, but he knew she was not going to stop until he was by the passenger station. Sixty pounds of air does not have the stopping power of ninety.

He kept the whistle going, to warn them he was coming. The yard force heard, but few of them had an inkling as to what was going on until it was too late.

First No. 2 had already come. The engine had gone to the roundhouse, and the switches were lined for No. 1 main. When he was almost by the crossover leading into No. 2 main, the yardmaster came alive to what was happening. He dashed in, lined the crossover that threw the runaway train away from the standing Pullmans, but it threw them squarely into the face of the official train, with the general manager's car, the president's car, and two Pullmans carrying the board of directors and their families!

Bill was running five miles an hour when they hit. The official train was doing less than that. The two engines came together with a resounding smack. Their pilots crushed like toothpicks. The two boilers cracked heads, and shattered glass flew far and wide.

Men came running, some from the yard office, some from the roundhouse and the town. Disheveled brass hats, rudely awakened from slumber, poured out from the private cars demanding to be told what was going on.

The old block—Vice President Wellington himself, in pajamas, bedroom slippers, and a bathrobe—was not the last one heard from. Shivering in the snow, his false teeth clicking with cold and fear, he declared the man responsible for that indignity must be discharged.

King Lawson heard the straight of it while the big hook was cleaning up the yard. He invited all concerned to be present when he tried the case. A humbled Duke Wellington pleaded guilty. A choleric parent himself passed sentence.

"You," he stormed, "are going to work on the end of a pick-handle till you learn a little sense!"

There were smiles on railroad faces when the rawhider slunk away in disgrace, and joy in railroad hearts.

Lawson came through the caboose down by the viaduct that

night where Kiamichi Bill was once more studying with his private teacher.

"That's right, old man," he encouraged. "Get yourself in trim, for you're going to get another chance next week to establish conductor's rights."

After Lawson had gone, Lula rumpled Bill's hair and said: "It won't be long now, kid." And Bill answered with a smile: "It won't be long."

Kiamichi Bill's story
concludes in "Death Traps"

Death
Traps

I

The Dreaded Doors

AT one time or another every railroad in the United States has had along its lines a string of trainmen's death traps. Most of them, like the coal chutes set close against the main line at Borden, have been stationary. The rest have been on rolling wheels; but whether stationary or rolling they have been eliminated only after long and bitter struggles between the men whose lives they endangered and the company whose money must be spent in the process of elimination.

Of those on wheels, the side door caboose has been among the most dreaded by the men who ride the iron. The S. & S. had twenty good ones.

When rolling wheels had made too many wives widows and called too many conductors on the last long run, the states in which they were used on branch lines outlawed them. But instead of shoving them off into the Mississippi or coupling them together and having a bonfire, Old Bull Horgan, who ran the S. & S. and carried the legislature of his own state in his vest pocket, brought them into Springvale and had them assigned to main line service.

"Kiamichi" Bill Burns was parlor man then on Frank Spalding's chain gang car, and they drew one of the side doors. They had registered in on merchandise and were going home to clean up for a party Mrs. Spalding was giving the new trainmaster when they found the notices in the mail box in the yard office.

Spalding read his first. He swallowed his Adam's apple a couple of times, looked at Bill with something in his eye which had not been there an hour before and said with a short laugh:

"So they're taking our platform buggy away from us and giving *us* one of the outlaws. I thought — "

Spalding shut up like a clam. A wise man seeking official approval did not criticize too severely the acts of men who could bestow the approval.

Kiamichi was not seeking official preferment. He made uncomplimentary remarks about the pedigree of certain high men and declared hotly: "I'm not going to take this lying down, Frank. I've had that 641 ever since I've been on rear end."

"But you don't own it, my boy," Spalding soothed him. "You only *use* it. These cabooses belong to the railroad company."

"I don't give a hang if they do. I've fixed this one up with my own hands. I've built in lockers and closets and worked on it till it's the sweetest buggy on the whole system. I'm going in and protest to Mr. Lawson."

Although the conductor refused to join him, the brakeman protested to the superintendent. Not because it was equipment dangerous to the life of the man who works it, for Bill had not yet learned from experience that it was. He protested because the 641 was "my caboose; I've had it five years, and I don't want to give it up."

Of course his protest did no good. Superintendent Lawson explained that the change had been made, not primarily by him, but as the result of orders from on high.

"Since we have to make it," he said, I'm signing the outlaws to the youngest conductors in point of service. That's the only fair way to do it. Spalding gets one. I regret it fully as much as you fellows. Mr. Horgan does not feel he can afford to junk several thousand dollars' worth of good equipment. There's nothing I can do about it."

"I suppose there's nothing we can do about it, either?" Kiamichi squinted at the superintendent.

Lawson smiled just a little.

"I wouldn't want to be repeated in this, Burns, because it *might* be only a rumor. But I *heard* that down in Arkansas the four railroad Brotherhoods cornered some politicians and told them there was another election coming some day; and the politicians outlawed the side doors there. That, I understand, is why we have them back here now."

The brakeman was gaining prestige in the trainman's Brotherhood. He grinned broadly and said: "Thanks, Mr. Lawson. It might pay our order to investigate that rumor."

IN the sweltering heat of an August afternoon the conductor and brakeman came to the freight yards to move into their new waycar. It was shaped like an ordinary box car with a cupola atop one end. There were two narrow wooden steps underneath the narrow door in the center of its side, and curved grabirons reaching up on both sides of it. But even the new paint and the new white number stenciled in where the old one had been changed did not conceal the fact that it had been in service for many years.

Bill was on the point of mentioning this fact when he noticed that the conductor, instead of swinging up to the narrow step and unlocking the door, had set his grip on the step and was rubbing his hand over a carving covered with red paint.

"Find one of the dates Noah, cut in this old ark?" he asked

sarcastically.

Spalding did not say a word, but just turned around and stared at him with a look of pain and surprise.

Kiamichi let the bag fall and caught him by the shoulder.

"What is it, Frank?" he asked anxiously. "What's eating you?"

Spalding swallowed hard and said: "I cut that initial there with my pocket knife sixteen years ago."

"Well, what of it? Didn't you know this old trap was killing trainmen when Cleveland was President?"

Spalding was getting a grip on himself by this time.

"That's just it, Burns," he said slowly. "This was my father's old caboose. He missed his step and went under it the very night I carved that initial."

But when Bill urged the conductor to ask the office at least to exchange this outlaw for another free from the taint of unhappy recollection, the conductor laughed shortly and answered:

"What's the use? I'm not superstitious. I'll ride this old buzzard till it shakes to pieces just to show it that I can."

They took over the 094 and fixed it up inside. It was not uncomfortable. The cupola and bunks had good cushions, and there was plenty of locker room and storage space for the mass of journal brasses, coupling pins and knuckles, chains, and repair tools which every freight caboose must carry.

At the time he became accustomed to catching the sidedoor arrangement of steps, he did not notice that it was more hazardous than the platform had been. Indeed, it isn't—when the man makes good his catch. But if he falls, the story is entirely different.

From the rear platform he will land in the track behind the wheels; he may break a rib or skin his nose and get up swearing. But when he misses the side door two wheels rolling relentlessly over an iron rail are his lot.

Bill broached the subject to the conductor. Spalding talked

freely about it. He told Kiamichi it was the howl raised by the men when the death trap killed his father that caused the side doors to be pulled off the Oldberg Subdivision and scattered to the branch lines.

"Then let's raise a new howl and have them pulled off again before they kill another man," Bill urged.

"I'm afraid a howl wouldn't get us anywhere, now," Frank said with a shrug.

"Why not? The organizations were not as strong then as they are now."

"Neither was Bull Horgan. He was division super here then. He pawed the air and tore up the earth when the men went to bat with it — swore the side doors were no more dangerous than the platforms, and swore he'd fire every man that signed the petitions. He fired a lot of them, too, not for that, of course, but on other pretexts. It's always been a sore spot with him that the men ran it over him. I have a hunch that's why he brought all of them back to this one district."

BILL had learned to fight since he had joined the ranks. He and his buddies had been fighting years to secure the removal of certain stationary death-traps, such as the coal chute at Borden, and some loading platforms along the line, and an overhead bridge at Big Catalpa. He determined then to start a scrap which would not end until the last side door car had gone into the graveyard. He urged the conductor to join him.

"Not me," Spalding told him. "You fellows go fooling around here, gouging into that old sore in Bull Horgan's gizzard, and you'll find yourself walking down the right-of-way carrying a suitcase."

Kiamichi did not insist. He knew why the conductor was refusing, and it filled him with a feeling of disgust.

Spalding was an ambitious young chap, keen-minded, energetic, a good mixer and a hard worker. His wife, Marie, was a queenly brunette with the dash and charm which made her the wife to go all the way with him — while the going was up. With her playing the social end and his working like a dog, they fully expected to pull the wires which would take him away from cars and cabooses and set him in a swivel chair.

When Bill had married Lulu Ross, shortly after Frank had come on the car, the Spaldings had kindly volunteered to show them around and help them get their start on the upward climb. But Kiamichi had no hankering for stiff hats and swivel chairs. His way up the iron road was plainly marked — consist, wheel report, and switchlist in the foreground, blending gradually into the gold braid and brass buttons of some passenger train far out on the sundown trail.

While Frank had been playing to the office, trying to lift himself from the ranks, Bill had cast his lot with the Brotherhoods, furthering the right of the working man to life and a living wage. He was now on the local grievance committee as an active organization worker. He urged his local to file formal protest against the use of the side-door cars.

The case went up to the throne. The reply came back in a curtly worded refusal which read in part: "Records of accidents on these cars fail to show that they are more hazardous than other equipment. Such being the case, the management is not inclined to discard them because of prejudice. For the present, at least, employees will continue using the equipment assigned ... "

Spalding laughed a little when Kiamichi told him how the case turned out.

"I told you you wouldn't get to first base with it," he said with just a hint of superiority. "Old Bull Horgan will make us use these things here till the wheels roll out from under them before he'll give them up."

"I think not," Kiamichi said stubbornly. "We're not quitting the fight just because we lost the first brush."

The case went into the hands of the general organization, which was then fighting over the Union for state laws to protect the men. It turned the case ever to its lobby in the state legislature. This same lobby had been framing a "Dangerous Structures" act for every session of the legislature for ten years, only to have it turned down. It now framed a bill and had it presented at the opening of the session in January. Bull Horgan took the legislature out of his vest pocket and told it what to do with the bill. It was killed the last day of January.

Again Spalding scoffed out his I-told-you-so. This time Bill's temper flared.

"I should think *you,* " he said significantly, "of all the men on this system, would be helping *his* fellows instead of — "

The conductor was grinning. "I can't afford to risk losing my standing with the office."

"A hell of a lot of good a standing's going to do you once you miss your step on that old waycar."

IT was a bad winter in the Ozarks, with plenty of snow and ice, and temperature hovering around zero. The line had been tied up since the Christmas rush. In February the sun began working on the accumulated snow and ice, turning them into slush during the afternoon; but at night, when it had gone down, the crust froze over, and ground and platform wore a coating of glare ice.

That's the kind of weather which used to send men scurrying up the seniority lists. They all knew it; and they filled their shoes with spikes to guard against slipping.

Spalding and Burns were called out of Springvale on an oil train that morning at 10:30. The sun was shining from a sky of deepest blue, and the thaw had set in.

Trainmaster Serle, in high-topped boots and mackinaw, was bustling through the yards, directing and encouraging in an effort to break the traffic jam and get freight moving normally. He joined the crew while Baldy was reading the orders. When the engineer had finished, the trainmaster made them a little speech. Bill never forgot it.

"Fellows," he said, "I want you to make a special effort with this train today. This oil's due in St. Louis right now; but every cockeyed thing that could happen to a train's happened to this one except that it hasn't gone into the ditch. The oil company's burning up the wires telling the old man what they're going to do with their business front here on out if we don't make better time with their products. We want you to put it into Oldberg as soon as safety will permit, and we're going to help you all we can."

"We'll make use of all the help you give us, won't we, Baldy?" The conductor grinned.

"You betcha!" the big engineer answered. "We'll kink the rails and scorch the ballast if you say so."

"I know you will," the trainmaster assured them. "That's why I'm telling you. I can depend on you fellows to get over the road with a train when you have a chance."

"Thanks, Mr. Serle," Frank answered with a gleam of pride. "We feel like we're paid to move trains, not to keep them standing on sidings."

"That's the system, Spalding!" The trainmaster clapped him on the back. "I wish all our conductors felt that way about it."

They had one of the new decapods that day. A year ago Baldy had been calling them white elephants. Then no engineer could get them over the road, and no one wanted to.

Now they had become the real thing. Firemen had learned to operate their mechanical stokers, and engineers had learned to make them eat up the miles. Officials had learned that if they wanted freight at the other end of the line, all they had to do was put a man like Baldy Elkins into the cab of a decapod, hook light tonnage to its tail, and keep it out of sidetracks.

That's the way things stacked up for that trip. Every man in the crew was on his toes because there was the promise of a short day and easy money. They were running as Extra 44 and had thirty-two cars — less than half the engine's tonnage rating. Baldy stepped out of town with it like a passenger train,

They intended to make Roaring River, sixteen miles east, for a meet with No. 1; but the dispatcher had the board out for them at Danville. Kiamichi, watching from the cupola, called the color to the conductor, who was working on reports.

Spalding shouted: "Grab it, will you? He's probably letting us go to Allenby for them."

He was. Bill glanced over the tissue and read aloud that No. 1 would wait at Allenby until 12.01 P.M. for them.

"Giving us ten minutes," Bill commented.

"Not much, but enough to go on," Spalding said with a glance at his watch.

When Baldy whistled for Roaring River, he had running time and six minutes. The rules required ten; but he whistled that he was going through.

Bill shouted down to the conductor:

"Do you want to go over?"

"Sure!" Spalding shouted back. "Baldy will make up three or four minutes on the hilt."

Bill waved a timetable out of the window. The engineer answered. And the conductor guessed right. With the light train, Baldy went to Allenby in four minutes less than regular running time. He had plenty of time to get into clear when he started heading in, but he went in pretty fast because he wanted to inspect the engine and let the men look over their train.

BILL was standing in the door, watching the tanks go through the switch. When sixteen had passed, he saw snow and water fogging from the track ten cars ahead.

He did not know what the cause was, but he leaped inside, opened the conductor's valve, and set the brakes. It was well he did. Baldy whistled out the flagman. Bill ran to the switch. A chunk as big as his head had broken out of a wheel, and it had left the track and taken the tank of gasoline with it. The derailment had torn up the switch and spread the track for a distance of fifty feet. The wrecker crew brought the big hook from Springvale; and men, wading through slush and snow, rerailed the car and repaired the track. And when the sun went down, the slush froze, and the ground became slippery.

By the time the track was repaired, it had been dark an hour. Clouds had annulled the stars; and a wet snow was falling. Three passenger trains were lined up to meet them and two were waiting behind them to pass. They left Allenby at 8.05.

The little wreck had spoiled an easy day, but it had not spoiled the crew's morale. When they pulled out of Allenby, they were still on their toes, still working together like the spokes of a wheel, and still figuring on getting their oil train into Oldberg as soon as safety would permit.

Baldy made another good run. He covered the seventy-five miles to Skunk Creek in two hours and twenty minutes, and stopped at the tank at 10.28. Because he lacked a few minutes of the time required to go to Dripping Springs for No. 9, he intended to head in at Skunk Creek for it.

But the dispatcher was on his toes, too. He was still trying to get that oil train into St. Louis, and he had some orders out for them at Skunk Creek.

It was snowing so hard they could not see the board, but Spalding expected it to be red. He did not wait until they pulled up the line to see. When the train stopped, he hurried over to the office, and on the way he fell twice on the snow-covered ice. He got a "31" order instructing him to meet an extra at Dripping Springs, and a "19" order telling him that No. 9 would wait for him ten minutes there. Signing for the "31," he took both orders to the engine.

"Do you want to try to go up there on that time?" he asked. "Dispatcher said if you didn't go to let him know so he could pass it to them at Dripping Springs."

"Sure I'll go on it," Baldy answered, "provided I don't have to wait for the conductor to catch the caboose pulling out."

"Don't worry about me, old bean," Spalding assured him. "When you get ready to go, you can leave town."

THERE was a long platform at Skunk Creek. It ran ten car lengths toward the caboose. When Spalding left the cab, he looked back up, as if he considered riding the engine.

"You better come back and ride with us," Baldy advised. "When we leave here, we'll be goin' out like a string of turpentined monkeys headin' for the jungle."

"Go right on!" Spalding called back. "Highball!"

Baldy whistled off; the oil tanks started away; and Frank Spalding hurried to the end of the platform. If he had expected to find this lower end dry like the upper, he was mistaken. The drip from the eaves had been draining down all afternoon: It had settled in low places in the board, and an inch or more of snow had fallen on it.

Spalding had not yet learned how fast Baldy Elkins could start sixteen hundred tons out of Skunk Creek with one of these big engines. By the time he had reached the end of the platform he knew it was a lot faster than he had expected. When twenty cars had gone by, the train was moving so fast he would not dare try to catch an oil tank.

He was not a nervous man, but when the marker was five cars away, his heart was tying knots in his necktie. If it had not been snowing, he probably would have signaled the engineer to stop rather than to take the chance. But it *was* snowing, and the only way to pass a signal through the snow would be for Bill to pull the air, and set the brakes, and that would stick them here for No. 9. Spalding clamped his teeth, buttoned his coat, and stood waiting.

Bill was always uneasy when the conductor had to catch that caboose running too fast. He did not know why. Maybe it was because he could see the ghost of Green River Spalding stretched ever athwart the threshold of that old side door. Tonight, when Baldy sent the two long blasts wailing through the storm, telling Skunk Creek he was going east, Kiamichi muttered:

"I sure hope Frank rides the cab."

He hoped it still more fervently as the click of the wheels came faster and the cry of flanges rose to a stream. He watched anxiously. Soon he saw the gleam of a light through the snow. It disappeared and came again.

With a muttered "Damn fool!" he grabbed the broom and swept accumulated flakes off the step and wiped the grabiron with his glove. Then he backed away to give the conductor room and watched with bated breath.

When the caboose came on, Frank leaned forward, lantern on his arm, and took the iron with both hands. As his hands connected, something happened. It looked as if a foot slipped, or maybe both feet. Then his hands slipped. The lantern went down into the track, and after it the man.

Bill hurled himself to the floor on his stomach, clutching for his buddy, but he never had a chance. Before he could so much as find a shred of clothing, the conductor had gone under, screamed once and disappeared in the darkness.

Leaping to his feet, Bill darted to the cupola and opened the brake valve. He did not wait for the train to stop, but jumped off and raced back. He was talking fiercely, saying things he did not mean and not aware he was saying them.

He fully expected to find the conductor cut into a thousand

pieces. He thought many a time afterward it was too bad he wasn't. But with some instinctive twist of the body Spalding had whirled as the wheels came on, and had almost cleared the rail — almost but not quite. The car had been moving a little too fast.

On a platform car he would have swung behind the last wheel and got a few skinned spots, or even a broken bone. On this car — well, two wheels had passed over his right arm and leg.

Chapter II

"Make Him Keep His Trap Shut!"

THAT accident brought many changes on the S. & S. These changes mattered little in the world as a whole, but they mattered much in the lives of those concerned.

Frank Spalding had been a good man, company man; but that made little difference when the time came for settlement. The company offered to pay his hospital fees, to give him a few hundred in cash, a lifetime pass, and a lifetime job flagging a crossing. Spalding accepted the surety of the company settlement rather than to chance the uncertainty of fighting; and when he was able, he went flagging the Main Street crossing, hobbling around with a crutch held under the stub of an arm because there was not room to fasten a cork leg and make it work.

His had been a strong personality. Except for his zeal in hastening the movement of traffic, and the death trap, he would have gone far in the railroad world. But when the human body is crippled the mind often becomes dwarfed and crippled, too. That's what happened to Frank. As Kiamichi watched him hobbling along out there through rain and shine, he knew a human life was disintegrating like a dike of sand on a flooded river; and his heart went out to the man whom the road had maimed.

Mrs. Spalding went to pieces, but, though she would have denied it, not out of grief for her husband. With little money to give parties and shine among the other lights of which she had been one of the most brilliant, she was lost. To find companionship and pleasure, she began stepping out with other men — men who had money.

Frank grew suspicious, then certain, and finally offered her liberty. She accepted it, and tried to brace up, but it was pleasant and easy to keep on as she had started. And then, somehow, her social ambitions became less important, and her life began to disintegrate, too.

Some scorned and censured them, and then forgot them. Kiamichi could do neither. His heart wept for them, and he burned with a fierce anger at the system which sacrificed their lives.

Spurred on by him and others like him, the Brotherhoods had entered another and stronger protest to the management. They had pointed out that this accident was one of those things which might be anticipated as long as the side door caboose was equipment on the company's lines.

This protest, like the other one, seemed to stir up all the venom in the soul of Old Bull Horgan. He sent back a curt refusal, and called attention to the facts brought out in the investigation — the facts on which the company would have based its defense had Frank brought suit for injury. "That company rules forbid men taking chances; that the employee in question had taken a chance in attempting to board the train which was traveling at too great speed; that the equipment was not to blame, but the man's judgment."

Bill and his friends were bitter now, for despite the fact Frank had been a company man, he had been very popular. They declared they would not give up the fight until the legislature had passed laws, not only to forbid the use of side door way cars, but also to compel just settlement for injury received by employees in the line of duty, regardless of who was to blame.

AT first his efforts caused no more stir than a pebble tossed into a stormy sea. But as months went by, he began to feel a growing power. New contacts and new requirements were bringing out a gift for oratory which even his best friends had not suspected. Talking in lodge hall, in sandhouse, in hotel lobby, he said things which finally reached the offices where the big brass hats sat.

Old Bull Horgan came to Springvale. Oh, no, he did not make a special trip. He just dropped in casually to talk with Superintendent Lawson.

"Who is this man Burns?" he asked.

Lawson squinted calculatingly through the smoke. "You mean the emergency conductor, Bill Burns?" he asked, though he knew very well whom he meant.

"I mean the Burns who's been shooting off his face about the inhuman management of this company, about keeping death traps for freight cabooses, and about how when a man walks into one of them, we turn him out to starve."

A bulldog growl was there, but Lawson had a big juicy chunk of steak ready.

"Do you recall, Mr. Horgan," he asked placatingly, "an evening five or six years ago when we were riding the motor car over from Springvale to Oldberg — "

"And almost hit a freight caboose below Dripping Springs?"

"Yes, sir," Lawson nodded.

"I should say I do. I also remember you never did fire anybody."

"Burns is the hobo kid who stopped those runaway cars and kept them from ramming us and killing — "

"You mean to tell me that blanket stiff you picked up and made a brakeman of is the fellow that's raising all this hell with us? Why, damn his ungrateful hide! He ought to be kicked off the job and blackballed."

"Fortunately, Mr. Horgan," Lawson said significantly, "ingratitude is not an offence for which man may be punished. Burns has proven a very capable and efficient trainman."

"Who gives a damn how capable and efficient he is? I want you to call him in here and burn him up. You remind him that he is in the service of this company, and that he must respect its officials. You make him shut his trap and keep it shut."

"But — "

"Don't argue with me, Mr. Lawson. I'm giving you final instructions. You and that trainmaster of yours make Burns keep his trap shut about this side door caboose deal, or else you find something to fire him for. If you don't, I'm going to put men in here who will."

BILL BURNS had passed his conductor's examination and been promoted for a year when Spalding had been injured. But passing an examination does not place a man in charge of a train, and neither does efficiency. Seniority does that in the course of time.

For a while after he is promoted, he continues to hold a regular turn braking on freight or passenger crew. During that time he is an "emergency" conductor. Kiamichi remained on the emergency list, running when he had a call, braking when he didn't. Older conductors died off, were discharged, or resigned. He moved slowly up the list.

Shortly after Horgan had his talk with Lawson, the fall rush started. New crews were put into the freight pool. Everybody moved up a few notches, and Burns went up to extra conductor. As such, he gave up his regular turn braking and was marked on the extra board, where he worked with other extra conductors, taking his turn when it came due.

About this time Superintendent Lawson had a talk with him

and offered a bit of friendly advice.

What's the matter?" Bill asked shortly. "Getting under some-body's hide?"

"I'm not saying," Lawson told him. "But if I were in your place, I'd take it easy. Your job will probably last longer."

Burns frowned. Lawson had always been friendly to him, and friendly to the cause of the men. When Spalding had been hurt, Lawson had issued a bulletin warning trainmen to use extra care in boarding trains carrying side door cabooses and urging them not to attempt to do so while the train was moving rapidly.

Bill did not know it, but Old Bull Horgan had taken that as a slap at himself, and had censured Lawson for playing to the whims of the men, instead of backing up his superiors.

He asked: "You're not threatening to fire me for using my tongue, are you, Mr. Lawson?"

Lawson shrugged and played with his watch charm.

"I'm not threatening, Burns," he said slowly. "I'm just advising. After all, you must remember that you are working for a company; and that in the last analysis the management has full authority to designate the type of equipment until the type is specified by law or agreement."

Bill was not the man to be bullied or bluffed; but he had a deep respect for Lawson, and could see the logic in the super's advice. He did not talk so loudly nor so often for a while, and might never have done so had it not been for the cinder embank-ment at Cowles.

A few days after the conference the trainmaster moved out, and Big Bill Blankenship came in over the Oldberg Subdivision. Blankenship was Old Bull Horgan's son-in-law. Like Horgan, he had come up from the ranks, having started twenty-odd years ago as a switchman. It was whispered when he came in from the Plains Division that Horgan was greasing the skids for King Lawson and intended shooting Blankenship up to the superintendency as soon as he had time to learn the ropes on the Hill Division.

Blankenship knew his railroads, all right. There was no question about that. And he knew his men. He would neither countenance inefficiency nor play favorites.

Blankenship had a son named Eddie of whom both he and Horgan were proud. Both had their hearts set on making a railroad official of him just as soon as he learned a few things and became old enough.

When Eddie had finished high school and came out a slender youth of seventeen he looked like anything but a railroad official to them. He couldn't growl nor talk hard; his curly light hair did not bristle; his blue eyes laughed instead of glowering. But the two men determined it was time to put him out on the railroad, not only to learn the game, but to go through the hardening process they thought was necessary.

Certain he would prove to be a natural born railroader, they elected him to go braking instead of wasting his time in a college course, and so Blankenship hired him on the Oldberg Subdivision. He did not take to it as his parents had expected; he cared little for flagging, or tying down brakes, or packing hotboxes, or running for switches on a hill.

BILL BURNS began to hear about him shortly after he had marked up on the extra board. Officials' sons always come in for a lot of gossip, especially if they don't do so well; but it was the middle of September before they met.

They were called for a made-up crew out of Springvale. To get together such a crew the caller picks the man first out on the conductors' extra board and the two first out on the brakemen's board; and the yard force then grabs any kind of old caboose, no matter what, sticks it on the end of a train, and highballs the whole works out of town.

That night Kiamichi Bill drew Eddie Blankenship and another

student named Sanders along with one of the old side door
cabooses. The point was not covered by rule, but the understanding was always that the man first out on the brakeman's board
had the preference of working positions, with the more specific
understanding that the conductor on the crew could place his men
where he pleased.

Well, Eddie Blankenship was first out on the board that night.
That gave him the preference; and he went back to the caboose
to work the rear end. The rear end job is a responsible one, because
when anything happens and the conductor has to go forward on
the train the hind man is left in full charge. It was a tough initiation for Eddie.

Aware that both men were students and not reckoning one to
be much better than the other, Bill did not interfere when the
trainmaster's kid came back to take charge. Eddie did very well
getting out. He cleaned and hung his markers, filled and lighted
the lanterns, arranged his flagging equipment where he could get
to it. Bill didn't even have to tell him to go over the train and let
off the brakes.

They got out at dark on a drag with one of the stoker engines
and a man who didn't know how to fire it in a fog so thick you
could cut it with a knife; and they began having trouble right away
after they left Springvale. No steam, no speed. They went into
the hole at Roaring River to let a stock train-by them, and doubled
out.

Bill knew there was another extra following them, but he
didn't know how far behind. He told Eddie:

"Now, Blankenship, you set ten good brakes on this rear end
as soon as we stop. Don't just set them. Bleed the air brakes off,
and then tie them down tight with a club. When you get that done,
you go back down the hill and look out for that extra. You don't
need to go very far here, because they won't be burning up the
railroad dragging this hill. Go down far enough to stop 'em, and

stay till you're called in."

Eddie smiled his angelic smile, cracked his heels together in military fashion, lifted his hand in a salute and said: "Righto, Captain Burns!"

Bill chuckled softly. Despite the fact he was Old Bull Horgan's grandson, he was a likable chap.

Not realizing the need of haste, even though Bill had told him to hustle, Eddie did not hurry too fast, He was only seventeen and had never had any responsibility. When Burns was gone, he took a drink of ice water, fooled around a bit, and then sauntered out to set the brakes.

When he was bleeding off the first car, he noticed that the brake was set in emergency — set more tightly than he could possibly set it with a club. He looked at three cars ahead. They were all set the same way. He figured Bill was trying to rawhide him, and not realizing that the air brakes might leak off within a short while, he went on back down the hill flagging, and set not a single hand brake.

No, the train did not get away. Bill made a quick double, and had the engine coupled and the air cut in within twenty minutes. He then went back to let of the brakes he had told Eddie to set. When he found the job had not been done, he was furious. He had always tried to do his work, and figured everybody else, even a trainmaster's son, should do the same.

When Eddie came in from flagging Bill talked to him. But he didn't get hard about it — just told him impressively that air leaks out of brake cylinders and turns wheels loose to roll, and reminded him that if they had happened to get a car off the track running into Allenby, or had been otherwise delayed, the train might have got away down that hill and caused a million-dollar wreck.

EDDIE didn't make a snappy comeback, but simply turned a bit red in the face and went into the caboose. When they went into the hole at Allenby he looked the train over without being told; and Bill thought maybe the incident had been a good lesson for him.

The track goes through quite a sag between Allenby and Gobi. Young engineers who don't know how to handle the slack in a long freight train often snap a knuckle or pull a drawbar when they start out of it. And so they broke in two that night, just as they started up, and the train stopped a half mile east of the crossing. Bill had to go forward again to see what had happened, and reckoning they might be there quite a while, he told Eddie in terms anybody ought to understand that "This fog's thick, and we're right down here in a hole. You go back your full half-mile and then some."

Eddie did not snap his heels together this time nor salute "Captain Burns." He picked up his lights and started walking rapidly. He should have counted telegraph poles, but he didn't do so; maybe he didn't even know that they run around thirty-eight to the mile. At any rate, he let his listless feet be the judge. When he thought he had gone far enough, he strapped two torpedoes to the iron a rail apart, returned what he guessed was halfway to his train, strapped another one down and waited.

Pretty soon Bill heard the extra whistling for the crossing. He was between two cars replacing the broken knuckle. He knew by the whisper of the exhaust that "Frog" Follonsbee was stepping along with the train. He backed out from between the cars to listen. When the extra didn't strike those guns right at the crossing, he knew the lead in Eddie's pants had stopped his feet too soon.

The engine came over the crossing. Bill's eyes kept getting wider, and his mouth came open. When the pilot wheels rumbled on the trestle a quarter-mile behind his caboose, he started talking to himself.

And then the first two torpedoes went off close together. Very close. Bill called Sanders, who was working between the cars.

"Get out of there, kid!" he called. "We're going to get hit."

Bill was reading every sound. The engineer shut off and started drifting. Pretty soon the wheel shot the third torpedo, and the engineer answered the signal. Kiamichi knew right then that Eddie had come alive to what he was up against. So had Frog Follonsbee. From the three successive whistled answers, he knew the youth was waving a red fusee and the engineer was using emergency air.

The extra slowed. Bill's heart went into his boots because he knew that the conductor is responsible for the acts of his brakemen. There came a hard bump. Cars rattled and banged, and the echoes whispered away into the fog.

Bill and Sanders hastened back. They expected to find the caboose torn up; but the extra had been a short one. When they reached the rear end, the engineer was down with his torch looking at the water leaking from the caboose barrel. Eddie was still standing by, holding the red light and the fusee. He was pale around the gills, and he wasn't laughing.

Kiamichi intended to give him a good dressing down; but Follonsbee was talking. Frog was an old engineer who had pulled Bill Blankenship when the trainmaster was freight conductor on another district, and he was now telling Bill's boy that it never pays to take a chance, especially in a fog and when a train is stopped in a hole.

Before Bill had a chance to say some hard things which he had on the tip of his tongue, the engineer commenced kidding.

"Reckon his old man will fire him, Burns?" he asked with a wink.

"He ought to." Bill didn't think short flagging was anything to wink about.

Eddie said: "I don't know whether he'll fire me or not, but he'll sure beat the devil out of me."

Bill eyed the youngster searchingly. Eddie was in deadly earnest. Frog Follonsbee grinned and asked significantly: "Do you ever forget to report things like this, Burns?"

"Gee, it would sure be swell of you if you would," Eddie suggested.

Burns was snapping the rubber band on the back of his train-book and fumbling with the pencil while he did some quick thinking. He knew that rules require all such incidents to be reported to the office, but he knew also that conductors often forget, especially in the case of new men. He snapped the book into his hip pocket.

"All right," he decided. "We'll not report it, but I won't take any more chances on your killing somebody on this hind end. You get over to the engine and let Sanders work the rear. See if he can shake the lead out of his pants and get his work done when we stop."

Eddie never uttered a word of protest. Maybe he figured it would do no good to protest because, as Kiamichi soon learned, Bill Blankenship was the kind of trainmaster who wouldn't play favorites, even with his own son. He set his red lantern inside the caboose, fished his lunch out of the grip and went forward to work the smoky end.

Chapter III

Not the Accident, but Its Tragic Result

SANDERS remained in the rear. He was an earnest, conscientious youngster, had grown up around the railroad, knew something about it, and was willing to learn and willing to work. They got along very nicely and had not a bit of trouble until they headed in at Cowles to let No. 6 by them.

Cowles was in the river bottom. The track going east out of it followed the river bank for a mile or more. The embankment

was steep, and a cinder path had been built up on the river side so the men could walk along their trains without falling into the stream twenty feet below. This path was almost level with the tops of the ties. But it was precarious, and it was constantly being filled in where it had washed down to the river.

Bill went to the door when Sanders dropped off to lock the switch. Conductors usually do, especially with new brakemen, because one of them is likely to get excited and lock a switch open with the red light staring him in the face. The train was running slowly, but Sanders had a little trouble with the lock, and the engineer had whistled off and started moving by the time he had done with it and started sprinting after the caboose.

He kept the middle of the track until he came even with the rear end. There he could have caught the side ladder, climbed to the top and come in through the cupola. He didn't do it. Nobody ever did. He swung off to the cinder path, and came up alongside.

He was running even with the side door and reaching out to catch the grabiron when it happened. As in the case of Spalding nobody ever did know exactly how, but everybody said lie must have got a foot too far out toward a loose cinder rim and that his foot kicked a chunk loose and started the whole path caving into the river.

Instinctively Sanders started grabbing for something as he went down — anything to break his fall and keep him from skidding down into the water. The first thing he found was the steel rail. That would have been all right if wheels hadn't been rolling over it; but with that side door car there were still two wheels to be reckoned with. Sanders didn't think about the wheels, for he didn't have time to.

They struck his hand — struck it just above the wrist joint. Bill heard the cry, saw his man go rolling toward the river, but he never once thought of what might have happened.

He pulled the air and went back to help him in case he got into the water. But a clump of thorn brush stopped him, and it was there Bill found him, groaning and crying with pain and misery.

The engineer, of course, had sent Eddie to see what had happened, Bill was administering first aid when he came in. He stopped at the door and saw and heard Sanders crying and Kiamichi swearing like a mad man — cursing Old Bull Horgan, and Big Bill Blankenship, and the board of directors; and the side door cabooses.

Eddie stared for a minute and his face went white. Bill looked up and saw him standing there gulping.

"Well, come in here and help me," he barked. "Don't stand there gapin'. An' while we're at it, just remember that if I hadn't sent you to the head end, it would have been *you* lying here crippled for life instead of *him.*"

Maybe Eddie thought Bill was wishing it had been he instead of Sanders. He didn't come to help, but backed out and started running. He never stopped until he reached the engine. The engineer came on the run. They backed into Cowles, cut off the caboose and returned to Springvale.

Sanders was a railroad widow's only son. His father, a freight fireman, had been annulled ten years ago when his train had sideswiped a string of box ears left too close to the track. Blankenship had hired him partially out of sentiment.

Bill never forgot the scene on the platform that morning when they arrived in the rain-washed dawn to put the boy into the ambulance. Superintendent Lawson had a telegraph set rigged into his home so he could listen in on the dispatcher's wire and know what was going on. He had heard of the accident and both he and Blankenship were there with Mrs. Sanders.

There was no weeping or wailing or recrimination. The boy joked painfully; the mother didn't say anything. She just tightened her hand on the trainmaster's sleeve and tried to smile.

Superintendent Lawson patted the boy's head and muttered: "That's the old system, kid. A railroad man knows how to take it standin' up."

The leaden ambulance whisked away through the rain. Lawson helped Mrs. Sanders into the car, and the train-master turned to his son. Eddie was standing by the caboose step his face white and his eyes all wet. Blankenship gave his trembling hand a fervent pat, and turned to swing into the car and drive away.

IT may have been the peculiar glint of moisture in the trainmaster's eye which caused Kiamichi to change tactics in his fight for elimination of death traps. Probably it was the fact that along with his zeal for the Brotherhood cause and his arguments for it he had imbibed its teachings in diplomacy. At any rate, instead of going to the throne now with blood in his eye, he talked to the other fellows and headed a committee waiting on the trainmaster.

Blankenship met them cordially, passed the cigars, and himself broached the subject which he must have known they had come to discuss with him.

"Burns," he began, "it's too bad about that Sanders kid. I sure hate it."

"Yes," Bill answered tightly. "It is too bad." There was a moment's Silence. Bill cleared his throat and tried to stifle the quaver which came when he remembered the morning at the ambulance. "I'm just wondering if, on the heels of this, we might get some action toward the elimination of dangerous equipment."

The lines on the trainmaster's face set. Evidently he knew about the fight which the men had waged. Maybe he knew why Bull Horgan was refusing to listen; and maybe he had his orders and knew what to do about it.

He flipped away the cigar butt, leaned back in the swivel chair, and gripped its arm with his big hands.

"We can't blame this accident on faulty equipment, Mr. Burns," he said a little harshly. "It is one of those unavoidable things which come to railroad men. We all know that hazards exist, and we agree to accept them when we seek employment with the company."

"There are unavoidable hazards, Mr. Blankenship, and will be as long as wheels roll over steel rails. This was *not* one of them. You know as well as I that these side door cabooses have injured five men."

"Come, come, now, Burns! You can't attribute this accident to a side-door caboose."

"The accident, no; the tragic result of it, yes," Bill came back swiftly.

"But your report — " The trainmaster found a clip of sheets containing the reports of the men who had been present. "According to these, the cause was the cave-in of the cinder embankment."

"The cave-in caused the fall, sir; but the maiming of the man was due solely to the fact that there were still two wheels to pass the point where he fell. If we had been carrying a platform caboose it not only wouldn't, but *couldn't* have happened."

The trainmaster lifted a hand.

"Wait a minute, Mr. Burns. Let's get our running orders straight. Because I'm in Mr. Horgan's family and because Mr. Horgan has so far refused to consider the elimination of what you choose to call death traps, you have come to me instead of going with your complaint to the proper official. Is that correct?"

Bill was forced to admit that it was.

"All right. Now let's understand something else. I'm a cog in the works of this machine. I'm working here under orders from my superiors, same as you are. Any complaints you have to take up must be taken up with the higher officials."

"Then we can't depend upon you to lend the weight of your personal influence to our cause

"Certainly not, Mr. Burns. My work is to keep men in line, to enforce the rules, and help move the traffic; not to determine the equipment which shall he used or the type of structures along the right-of-way."

Bill was reluctant to give up. "You have a son working here now," he said.

"I have thought of that, Mr. Burns," the trainmaster replied as he gouged a letter opener into a blotter. "I am *his* trainmaster, just as I am yours."

"And you would feel the same way if it had been Blankenship instead of Sanders?"

The trainmaster didn't look at the conductor. He kept digging into the blotter with the letter opener.

"Yes," he answered, when he had his voice under control. "Yes, I should still have felt the same. I knew when I hired him railroading he was going into a hazardous occupation. I accepted the responsibility. In fact," he added with just a trace of a smile, "when I first heard of the accident, I figured it was Blankenship instead of Sanders."

Bill started a bit, but before he could comment the trainmaster explained.

"I happened to know," he continued, "that Eddie was called out with you, and that he left here working the rear end. I did not know he had changed positions — no, I've not asked him or you why he did. That's your business and his, not mine."

"You still feel it was an unavoidable incident?"

"Regrettable but unavoidable."

"Then we'll go back into the fight, and if we fail to get action from the office, we'll go with it again to the state legislature."

"And I shall neither help nor try to hinder you."

Bill headed for the door.

"Thanks, Mr. Blankenship!"

"You are welcome, I assure you."

WHEN the conductor left the office, he was thinking that it would be funny if the trainmaster's son should be the next victim of official obstinacy. He wasn't wishing it and he wished instead that there might be no next victim; yet he knew there would be.

The organizations again petitioned the general office to discontinue the use of side door cabooses and to eliminate all trackside structures which would not clear a man on a freight car.

Again they were met with a flat refusal. They were told that the Sanders case, which occasioned the petition, was not due to faulty equipment, but to the fact that the man himself had been excited, and had fallen or was thrown down by the cave-in of a cinder embankment. Again they were told that every structure on the company's lines which would not clear a man on a car was plainly marked, and if an employee disregarded the warning, the fault was his, not that of the railroad.

The organization continued the fight. Injuries resulting from death traps on the S. & S. were cataloged. Kiamichi helped to gather the data. He sent pictures of the men who had been maimed, a photograph of Jack Sanders with a hay-hook where a hand ought to be, and one of Frank Spalding before and after.

He could not understand how any human heart could fail to respond. But so long as Bull Horgan controlled the legislature, all the pictures, tragedies, and lobbies in the world could do nothing. The lawmakers jumped when he cracked the whip and turned thumbs down on every piece of organization legislation presented.

Many of the men were passive. So long as they or their own sons were not involved, they took no active part in trying to remedy the situation. Most of them never gave a thought to the side-door caboose or to other death traps except when something happened. Then they only shrugged and wondered who would be the next victim. Every one figured, of course, that it could not possibly be himself — everyone except Eddie Blankenship.

Bill was out with him often that fall and winter. By the end of February he was developing into a fairly good man — nothing to brag about, but as reliable as the average.

He and Kiamichi Bill had become firm friends. The little hard feeling which had come from their first trip together had gone, and the Sanders affair acted as a bond between them. Often when they were called for the same run Eddie would stop in at the Burns' place and they would walk down to the yards together.

He stopped in that day in February and played with the baby while Bill was eating lunch. He knew of the effort which the Brotherhoods were making to insure the safety of railroad men, and he brought up the subject that morning.

He said, "It sure is too bad the legislature refused to pass that Hazardous Equipment Act."

"Yes," Bill agreed, "it is too bad."

Eddie was wrought up. He said:

"I don't see why gran'pop doesn't take these old side-door crummies off the road, couple them all together and shove them down in the Gulf of Mexico."

"That will be your job when you get to be general manager," Lula Burns said with a laugh.

"Believe me, I'll do it!" Eddie was in dead earnest. "I don't blame the fellows for not wanting to work them. I feel every time I'm called to ride one of 'em like I was taking the thirteen steps to the gallows."

Bill knew that was so. He had become aware shortly after the Sanders affair that Eddie was deathly afraid of them. Whether some of the men had suggested he ought to be the next victim, or whether the experience that night on the caboose at Cowles had struck home Bill never knew. He did know that when Eddie went to catch a step he would brace his feet and suck in his breath, and his eyes would get big as saucers; and more than half the time he passed up the side steps, caught the rear ladder, climbed to the top and went into the caboose through the cupola. A railroader, even a green student, won't go to that much trouble unless he's scared stiff.

Chapter IV

The Coal Chute at Borden

THEY got the 094, Frank Spalding's old caboose. It had been on the rip track again, and had come out with new paint and some new steps.

They left town at noon with ten cars of cattle, next the engine and thirty cars of oil and gasoline behind them. Dense gray clouds poured down a heavy snow which melted as it fell. When Bill caught the caboose pulling out of the yards his foot slipped and he almost went under. He came inside raving.

"You want to watch your step today, kid," he said to Eddie. "This man-killer's got its mouth open again." Eddie didn't say anything. He merely shrugged and went into the doghouse to read the orders.

"Whirlwind" Meyers was pulling them that trip. He was a good engineer, and he had a good engine. They had a hot shot train; but they didn't make hot shot time by any means. There were too many orders, too many passing tracks, and too many trains.

The legislature had just adjourned. The men who had defeated the Brotherhood measures, together with their hangers-on, were going home. They were riding Second No. 6. A lot of school teachers from the East were going to the coast to a convention, and they were riding four extra sections of No. 1.

The stock extra loafed along all that winter afternoon, heading into and out of sidings. The snow changed to a heavy downpour which left pools of slush with mush ice floating on it. Eddie went over his train every time they stopped, and Bill noticed that when he caught the side door, he took hold of the grabiron as if he feared it might get away from him.

As it was getting dark, they headed in at Big Catalpa to let First No. 6 by them. Second No. 6 was running an hour and ten minutes late. Kiamichi told Eddie as they pulled out: "We'll go down the main line at Borden and get our coal. If everything goes all right, we'll run along to Cowles to let Second Number Six by. If it doesn't, we'll head in the short track at Borden,"

It was twelve miles from Big Catalpa to Borden. There was a short grade pulling away from the Catalpa switch, and a curve a half mile out on the grade, where fifteen or twenty cars were visible from the cupola window.

Both men were in the doghouse, then, watching through the rain. When they were groaning around this curve, Eddie saw fire flying from a car somewhere ahead. Bill crossed the cupola and leaned over Eddie's lap to watch through the window. Soon a stream of sparks showed out of the darkness. It disappeared; then showed again, this time from several different positions.

"A sticking brake," Bill said disgustedly. "You can tell by the scattered sparks. If it was a brake beam down or a wheel off the track, the fire would be all in one place. It's probably a dirty triple valve that wouldn't let the brake release when Meyers kicked 'em off coming in here."

Expect I'd better hightail it over there and let it off before we get running any faster?"

"Might be a good idea. We don't want to burn up a pair of wheels and get fired for it."

"I'll say not."

EDDIE fished his lantern off the hook, went below and crawled into his wet slicker. When he was going out of the door Kiamichi called to him:

"You be careful now getting over those wet cars, and be sure you get the number of that baby so we can cut it out and report it."

Eddie made his way along the train, and the going was not particularly dangerous. There is a running board ten inches wide around the base of a tank car, and a railing made of iron pipe set waist-high for a man to hold to. He hopped nimbly along the boards, found the sticking brake, got down on his knees and held the bleed cock open until it released,

He did not try to cut the air out of it then. He intended to cut it out when they took coal at Borden, so he would not be bothered with it the rest of the way in. And he did take the number — KOSX 1582.

Since the train was not running more than eight or ten mites an hour, he didn't walk the boards back, it was easier to let the train run by him and catch the caboose. He jumped off and waited.

The track at that particular place was built on a steep embankment. He knew he could not have level ground to catch the caboose, but must stand on the grade and grab it as it came by.

Bill watched his lantern disappear in the cut. He never saw it again until he came through the cut and out to the high fill beyond. Beginning to grow uneasy, he had climbed down and come to the door. With the brake released, the train was now picking up speed, and the caboose was beginning to walk when it came by Eddie.

He was fidgeting around, trying to find footing on the embankment. He caught the grabiron with the right hand, held the lantern on the left arm, and reached for the step with his left foot. The foot found the step all right; and the hand with the lantern in it was groping for the iron back of the open door. But the hand didn't find the mark.

If Kiamichi hadn't been in the door, he would have gone down then. It would not have hurt him particularly, because on that embankment he would have taken a nasty spill instead of going under the wheels. When his foot hit the step it slipped from under him. Bill grabbed him by the left arm and helped him into the caboose. He was white and trembling.

"Phew!" he whispered. "That was a close one!"

"I told you you'd better watch this man-killer. She's out for brakeman's blood."

"She's not going to get any of mine tonight, cap," Eddie boasted. "From here on I'm going to catch that rear ladder, go high, and come in through the cupola."

He did. And that's what set him and Kiamichi Bill flirting with the undertaker over at Borden.

THE coal chute at Borden was one of the death traps which the men had been trying to eliminate. Years ago, when the road had come through, it had been built on heavy timbers set close beside the track. There may have been clearance for a man on the side of a car then, but with the widening of equipment that clearance had gone.

For years the men had been petitioning the management to move it back from the track before someone was killed. But the management had seen to it that signs had been put up bearing the warning that the structure would not clear a man on the side of the car. There had been a dozen men almost caught in it, but no one had yet been crushed to death.

When the extra stopped at the chute it was raining heavily and the night was black. Bill did not have to tell Eddie to look over his train. As soon as they stopped the youngster put on his slicker and struck out, looking for broken wheels and feeling for hot boxes. He never thought of his car with the sticking brake when he went up.

Halfway to the engine he met the head man. While they were exchanging greetings he remembered he had a brake to cut out on an oil car. He hurriedly crossed the train and came down the other side.

He found the KOSX 1582. He climbed under it, turned the anglecock which makes the brake inoperative, and bled it off. While he was doing this he noticed what looked like a crack in the arch bar, the support which carries the weight of the car upon the wheel arrangement. He examined it closely, and saw that the bar was broken almost completely in two.

"Wonder if it will hurt anything," he muttered. Then a moment later: "I think I'd better have the conductor come over and look at it."

He started on a run for the rear end because he knew the engine crew would soon be ready to leave town. Before he had passed five cars the engineer whistled off and started moving. Eddie did not take time to go over the top of the caboose that time. He caught the side door and ran in where Kiamichi was working.

Very briefly he described the break. "What do you think?" he asked.

Bill frowned. "I think," he said, "we're going to stop and set out a tank of gasoline."

Because the rear end could not signal the head end around the curves, he stopped the train with the conductor's valve. He did not know it then, but he stopped the crippled tank almost even with the coal chute.

Before leaving the caboose, he looked at his watch, studied his time card, and re-read his orders. It was now 7.42. Second No. 6 was due here at 8.20.

"We've got plenty of time," he said. "If we do have to set it out, we'll hold the main line, stick it over in the house track, and head in through the crossover."

Because Bill knew Eddie was going to the swivel chair and wanted to learn all he could of the railroad game, he explained rather carefully: "There's a slight grade west out of here. Not much, but enough to start a train roiling if the brakes all leaked off. We'll both be gone from the rear end, probably not long, but we never know. What should the hind man do before he leaves?"

"Set the caboose brake, and a couple more," Eddie answered promptly.

"Right. Do it."

The hand brake on a side door caboose is on top of the car, like a box car brake. Eddie went through the cupola window and set it while Bill was getting out the bill for the crippled car. He was starting for the oil tank to set another when Kiamichi stopped him.

"Don't bother about any more of them, kid," he said. "The

one will anchor them here till we come back."

THE rain poured down, and the men were wet and cold. While they were bleeding the brake so they could put the car away, the head man came back to see what was wrong. He and Eddie stationed themselves along the train to get signals to the engineer.

Bill rode the car into the house track, set the brake on it, and rode the rear end down to pick up the rear of his train. He did not think of the coal chute while he was riding back, because he was standing on the running board, not hanging to the side.

He connected the hose and cut in the air. He looked at his watch and knew they did not have time to go to Cowles ahead of second No. 6. He signaled ahead. Eddie was twelve or fifteen cars away, and that far from the chute. Eddie passed the signal and the engineer answered it.

Bill headed for the caboose to get out of the rain. The brakes had pumped up, and the engineer had started pulling the train through the crossover before he reached it. He went through the side door and started to fill out his delay sheet. He did not do it, because the caboose brake which Eddie had set was making a terrific clatter.

Then he went high through the cupola window to release it. It was tight, for Eddie had set it with a club, which Bill did not have. He put his lantern on the running board and put both hands to the task.

The train must have run four or five car lengths while he was working with it. They were down almost to the coal chute then. In the act of picking up his lantern after he had it released, he thought he heard something at the end of the car. He thought then it was Eddie Blankenship coming up the side ladder to dodge that step.

He didn't pick up the lantern, but instead flung a startled glance ahead. The coal chute was looking down with the flicker of a

moving lantern on its scarred and ugly timbers. The train was running five miles an hour straight toward it.

"Look out!" Bill shouted. "Don't catch it here!"

Then he whirled and, on his hands and knees, peered over the edge of the roof. Eddie had caught on and was starting his climb. Bill saw he could never make it.

This time he shouted: "Jump! The coal chute! It'll get you!"

Maybe the clatter of wheels and the squeal of flanges drowned his voice. Maybe Eddie was too startled to act. He looked up dumbly at Bill, then looked around at the timbers closing in on him, and started climbing. There was not a chance for him to make it. Maybe Eddie was too scared to know it, but Bill wasn't, He knew the boy could never get his body past the roof until it was too late, knew he was going to be crushed to a pulp between the car wall and the heavy timbers.

When they were yet a few feet from the first upright timber, Bill left the top of the caboose, caught hold the brakeman as he was going down, and tried to clear the timbers. He did not clear them. Both men crashed into the first upright. They did not go between it and the car, but they went down together and crumpled beneath the chute.

THE rolling death trap clanked by the fixed one. It curved through the crossover switch and stopped well down the short track. Because there was no hand to close them the switch points stood open. The switch light burned red; but the engineer could not see it until it was too late for him to stop, because the switch was on a curve.

Whirlwind Meyers received no signal that his train was clear. He never did. He had other ways of knowing when it had cleared. Realizing that he was stuck here now for Second No. 6 and for three sections of No. I, he went to bed. He had inspected his engine while the fireman was taking coal. He would get up when the trains went by to check their engine numbers and to answer signals. There was nothing else for him to do. He tucked his overcoat behind him, stuck his feet against the boiler head, and dreamed of a four-hour day on a railroad whose wheels were fixed so they couldn't turn in at a switch.

The head brakeman did not go back on his train to see whether or not it had cleared. It would have taken four men to pass a signal here from caboose to engine. He counted telegraph poles for the engineer in heading in, and told him when to stop. Without a worry, even though he had no signal, he set his lantern in the corner, cuddled down beside the warm boiler, and prepared to dry his clothes.

Back in the private dining car on the head end of Second No.

6, Old Bull Horgan was giving a banquet for the boys who had voted his way in the legislature. They had killed the Hazardous Equipment Act, which would have outlawed side-door cabooses and a few other rolling death-traps; the Dangerous Structures Act, which would have required the company to move back to a safe distance every structure along its rails which would not clear a man on the side of a car; the Full Crew Bill which would have forced the companies to put three brakemen on trains of more than forty cars; and a few other "pieces of tomfoolery" which the Brotherhoods had been trying to put through the legislature.

Baldy Elkins was wheeling Second No. 6. Superintendent King Lawson had come to him when they were leaving Springvale and told him to give the boys a ride, but not to throw the dishes through the window.

"The old man's on the line," he said. "He wants them to have a good time, and he wants us to put them through, because some of them have to catch the River Division Limited south out of St. Orleans."

"Okay, Mr. Lawson!"

Baldy was putting them through. He had the reverse hooked far up and the throttle far open, and he was taking the curves with an easy swing. The rain was spotting his front glass, and streaking down to fly back into the darkness.

Baldy whistled for the mile post. He did not need to whistle through, because he was on a train that owned the road. He was looking out for nobody, but everybody else was looking out for him. He expected to make St. Orleans at 2.40 without spilling the legislators into the cornfields.

He whistled for the mile post; and then he whistled for the crossing. Three of the usual four blasts rang out triumphantly; but the fourth did not come, for Baldy heard a sound and saw something flick under his headlight.

EDDIE BLANKENSHIP curled up under the coal chute and lay still. Bill rolled out where water dripping from the chute hit him in the face and when the wind blew, fine drops showered over him. It was cold, and he kept mumbling and muttering. He blinked at the inky sky, but he could see nothing except a thin crimson thread of light creeping under a warehouse and coal chute which hid them from view.

He kept wondering dazedly about that crimson thread, but it took him a long time to figure out whence it came. The water dripped incessantly into his upturned face, like a voice trying to arouse him. At first he thought he was with Frank Spalding, and that the crimson glow was the reflection of his light on a pool of blood. But that could not be it; years had passed since Frank Spalding had gone down under the wheels of the old side door.

That was it. A side door caboose — and Eddie Blankenship. Now he had it. Years ago, it seemed, Eddie had promised to get rid of the side door cabooses when he became general manager. And Eddie had said something about thirteen steps leading to the gallows. He blinked up into the darkness. From a reflected beam of light, he could see the uprights of a gallows — no, that was a coal chute. The Borden chute.

He wondered vaguely if Second No. 6 had passed. Then he knew it hadn't, because when Second No. 6 went by them, it was going through an open switch and slough into his caboose. They couldn't stop, because they would not know the switch was open until it was too late. And the switch was open. There had been no one to close it unless —

"Eddie!" he called. "Eddie!" But Eddie did not answer.

He tried to sleep again, but the rain would not let him. Instead, it hammered incessantly at the door of consciousness. They had been heading through the crossover at Borden. He remembered it all now. They had been going into the hole to let No. 6 by them, and Eddie had come up the ladder, had tried to come up the ladder, and the chute had been about to get him.

He was almost wholly conscious now. The rain in his face was driving away the fog. He knew he had to get back up the track and get a flag against Second No. 6. He knew it, but how!

He tried to get up, but he couldn't even stand. He groped and found an upright timber. When he tried to draw himself erect, his right leg crumpled under him. He knew then it was broken. He called Eddie again, but again there was no response.

All the while he kept trying to get up. He had not the slightest idea how long he had been there, but he knew Second No. 6 must be coming soon. He started crawling west along the track.

At first he had no plan, but as his head cleared he formed one. He had torpedoes in his pocket. He always carried them for emergency, not for anything like this, of course, but for emergency. He fumbled with a stiff, numb right hand and found one. Just one, but that was all he needed. One gun was a stop sign. If the engineer hit one torpedo he would stop.

When he had been crawling for a lifetime he knew the rails were snapping. Somewhere a train was running them. He could not hear it through the rain, but he knew it was coming.

Then he heard Baldy Elkins whistle one long blast. Then the crossing blast. The engine was close now. He strapped the torpedo to the rail and started crawling back, back toward the coal chute. That was the last he knew …

IT was a long time afterward that he saw Eddie Blankenship sitting in a drawing room with a bandage on his head, and heard him talking to Old Bull Horgan and some men he did not know. Bill could hear as plain as day what Eddie was saying:

"The coal chute — that was it. One of Bill Burns' death traps. It and a side-door caboose. You see, sir, we had had some trouble. I reckon I must have been excited and kind of forgotten the chutes. I had almost gone under catching the side-door steps, and I was going high on the rear ladder and running into it. When I was half way up, Burns yelled at me to jump. I couldn't figure what he meant until it was too late. When he saw I was going in, he must have thrown himself right down on top of me and taken me down with him. If it hadn't been for him — "

"And if it hadn't been for a stubborn old fool — " Bull Horgan's growl faded pleasantly as Bill went back to sleep. He was smiling dreamily, even though he was in pain. For he knew, vaguely but certainly, that the menace of trainmen's death traps was at an end on the S. & S.

WHEN Bill was called east again in the spring sunshine, he reported for duty on a steel under-frame caboose; and when he went down by the graveyard, he saw robins flitting through the unglazed windows of twenty side-door cabooses which had gone into the discard with the link-and-pin and the hickory club. Another victory had been added to the growing string of triumphs for the welfare of the men who ride the rails.

When the Devil Calls

A tale of the S. & S.

I

IT didn't take an ethnologist to tell that "Old Bill" Reardon wasn't Dutch. Even "Snakes" Thompson knew that much, and Snakey had baked his head in the heat of a fire-door until his brains had sizzled out like the juice from a toasted weiner. But neither Snakes Thompson, nor "Horseface" Harrison, nor any of the other boys on the S. & S., knew why William O'Reardon (as he was christened hack home in Ireland) had come to America and gone firing on the Western Division. That's something he hadn't discussed.

About all any of them knew or cared was that Old Bill could play poker and shoot craps and yank drawbars and whip freight trains around the Ozark curves better than any other hoghead on the Western; moreover, he wasn't afraid of anything under the sun.

Bill wasn't ashamed of his past. He hadn't attempted concealment. It wasn't that. He just had a hunch that he might be laughed at if he told his hard-boiled bunch that he had crossed the water to shake a family ghost off his trail.

Now this family ghost was no cause for mirth among the O'Reardons of Dundrum. For a dozen generations tandem ahead

159

of Bill it had been held in superstitious awe. Legend said it was the Devil himself whom one of the early ancestors had mortally offended. But legend was so badly muddled that it crossed itself and said this same early ancestor had helped the Devil out of a tight place and His Satanic Highness was trying to return the favor.

At any rate, during all those generations the master O'Reardon had been warned exactly when he was going to die. Not once, according to tradition, had this warning failed to come.

Several days beforehand, at the exact hour when death was due, the Devil or one of his imps would hunt out this particular O'Reardon and his legal heir together, cut loose with a hideous, mournful wail and end with just as many shrieks as the elder O'Reardon had days to live.

Some folks might think a warning like this would be a real favor. It would at least give a fellow a chance to say his prayers and wash his feet before he died, but the O'Reardons, by the time Bill came along, had begun to consider otherwise. They had come to think, after all these dozen generations, that His Satanic Majesty not only told a fellow when he was going to die but took particular pains to see that he died exactly when that time came. And they had some grounds for this belief, for every one of the dozen, so tradition had it, had died with his brogans on.

Consequently, since rum had gotten the property while the Devil was getting the souls, long before grass grew over the mound where the father was sleeping, Bill became the parent of a brilliant idea.

"Why," he asked himself, "can't I be leavin' this doomed country an' goin' across to Americy where the Divil can't foind me?"

The longer he mulled that idea over, the more thoroughly he became convinced that he could do that very thing and shake the evil spirit off the trail of himself and his descendants. It never

occurred to him that the Devil, *banshee*, or whatever the thing was which had been haunting the O'Reardons, could cross the sea the same as he could. In fact, he never worried about it until that night down at Rome.

II

A GREAT, dark cloud rolled its stilling curtain low over the wooded ridges and narrow valleys of the Missouri Ozarks. Oaks and pines showed black against the gray limestone cliffs, where the cone of brightness from the headlight of an eastbound freight swept over the hills.

The freight came creeping around Devil's Curve, and stopped at the west switch of Rome. The head brakeman, dropping off the pilot, opened the switch and the half mile of freight cars started clanking into the siding, to wait for four troop trains and a much delayed Number Six and Number Ten.

"Be here until daylight, won't we, Bill?" queried the fireman, crossing the cab and lifting his soot-blackened face toward the engineer.

"Yeah. Be here till the Devil starts peddlin' ice skates, so far

as I'm concerned," growled the hogger. "You put a good fire under
the old jack, Snakey, while we're gittin' in the clear; then you an'
me's headed fer the rear."

"Headed fer the hind end?" echoed the tallowpot.

"Exactly, boy. Old Horseface has got a bran'-new set o' ignorant dominoes back there. The head shack's jinglin' a pocketful
o' hot money an' Alkihol's got a quart o' good whisky an' fifteen
nice cattish he caught at Bloomfield. We're headed fer the crummy,
an' we're goin' fast."

Old Bill Reardon counted telegraph poles while the rail joints
clacked beneath him, counted until he knew his train had cleared
the switch. Snakey Thompson filled the firebox with green coal
and covered his headlight. Then the two of them struck out on a
run for the caboose, the engineer ahead.

Lightning laid a zigzag string of leaping fire from horizon to
zenith, then smothered it beneath a cloak of stifling blackness.
When the two men were halfway to the caboose, the wind struck
them. Powerful gusts hurled leaves and twigs from the neighboring forest, bent trembling trees until their branches all but swept
the earth. The men quickened their pace, striving to reach shelter
before the rain poured out its drenching flood.

In Horseface Harrison's caboose, the crap game was soon in
full swing. "Alki" Akers, always hungry and thirsty, started frying
catfish on the oil stove. While they sizzled, he took out the bottle,
which he passed from hand to hand around the table. He didn't
join the game. But Horseface and Snakey Thompson and Old Bill
Reardon and the head brakeman played it for all it was worth at
two bits a throw.

The game that night was a hot one. The click of dice on the
bare pine table came like the rhythmic *chuck-a-chuck* of a locomotive on a grade. The hard-boiled conductor with the three
fingers of his old link hand conspicuously absent and the ugly red
scar on the right side of his bespectacled lace conspicuously

present, glared across the hinged table at the jolly, tomato-face of the Irish engineer. Gently he caressed the celluloid cubes and talked to them darky fashion.

"Come on there, little girl. Don't you fool with me no more. That damn boghead's gittin' too—"

Lightning splintered a pine tree up on the hillside, and the crash that followed the blaze rolled from cliff to cliff until its echoes faded out into ghostly whispers.

"The old boy's shootin' at us, tonight, fellers," drawled the conductor, shoving the dice over toward Old Bill.

"Shootin's roight, Horseface," replied the engineer as he scooped the cubes into his spade-like hand and crooned to them for luck. "He's shootin' too domned close fer comfort."

He gave the hand a few deft twists, but paused just in the act of tossing the dice again upon the table. A weird, unearthly sound was coming into the caboose apparently from one of the windows, though so vague and shadowy was it now, it would be hard to say from exactly what spot.

At first it was a low wail, scarcely audible above the roar of the rain and the wind. Then it rose gradually and swelled in volume until it seemed to fill the caboose and even the whole valley. Now it sounded like a woman's frantic scream. Again, the voice of a little child crying in stark terror.

Finally, after what seemed to the listeners many hours, it ended with seven unearthly shrieks—like the fabled death shrieks of a condemned soul entering torment! Shrieks that left the five men clutching the table to steady tottering knees.

Horseface didn't count them, even though he was paid to do the head work for the crew, neither did Snakey Thompson nor Alki Akers. But Old Bill Reardon did. As the first low notes crept into the caboose, his nerveless hand unclasped, letting the dice fall to the table. Then his hands sought blindly, gropingly for the edge of the table and gripped until the nails had pierced the wood.

As the cry arose higher and higher, his blue eyes bulged. His crimson face turned gray. He stared unbelievingly, dumbly, like a dog whose master has just shot him, first at the conductor, then at the caboose windows, muttering again and again in a dry whisper:

"He's—he's found me! The Devil's—found me—here!"

And as the cry broke, he counted the shrieks, counted in that same loud, dry whisper, lapsing back into his brogue:

"Wan—two—thra—four—foive— six—sivin!"

III

THE storm was raging. Wind was roaring through the tree-tops; rain pouring down upon the tin roof of the caboose. The coal-oil lamp in its bracket above the table flickered and flared and all but went out. A troop train whistled away up in the cut, facing Devil's Curve, rolled around the long sweep of intervening track, and went thundering down through Rome.

Horseface, cynical, hard-boiled sinner that he was, was the first to recover from the shock. Reaching up into the unpainted pine cupboard, he took his delay sheet and jotted down the time of passage of the troop train—1:23.

Snakey crawled over to the side of the caboose next the main line and coiled up on the hunk. Alki, true to his nickname, stumbled to his locker, reached in, and, grasping the long-necked bottle, gulped down a half pint to shake the spell.

Bill Reardon stood waiting, listening, licking his dry lips. Stark terror was written in every curve of his gray face.

The conductor burst into a harsh, dry laugh. With a sneering grin more of bravado than of real courage, he turned to the engineer.

"Well, Bill," he began. "A feller'd think to look at you, yuh'd been drinkin' booze with the ghost uh your dead grandmother or shootin' craps with the Devil."

Bill made no reply. Smoke filled the caboose, acrid, pungent, stinking smoke from catfish burned to a crisp. Another troop train went thundering past. Snakey sat on the bunk watching the terror-frozen countenance of his engineer.

Finally, with a groan, Bill threw his arm to his face, reeled toward the front door, and went staggering out into the storm, followed by Snakey.

The two men made their way through rhythms of pitch blackness and blinding light back to the engine. Without a word they climbed to the cab, engineer and fireman sitting each in his own place. Coal smoke hacking out surrounded them, bearing with it a strong odor of brimstone. Bill seemed not to notice. Snakey turned on the blower.

The rain ceased. Dawn came creeping over the mist-enshrouded cliffs and across the dreary bottoms. Steam in the boiler wailed, moaned and cried. Air pumps panted and wheezed as they forced air back into the brake line to replace the leakage. The water gauge lamp threw out weird rays, furnishing the only light of the cab.

Snakey smoked one cigarette after another, glanced occasionally across the dingy cab where Old Bill sat, barely breathing. Finally, the engineer came wearily into the deck and stood leaning against the frame behind the fireman.

"Snakey!"

The fireman jumped. He hadn't known Old Bill was there.

"Snakey, did you hear that back there a while ago?"

Snakey tossed a half-burned cigarette out the cab window and gave a short laugh.

"I ain't deef," he finally countered.

"Did you know what it was, Snakey?"

"Naw, I didn't. Did you?"

"Snakey, I know what it was!"

"The hell you do!"

The fireman half turned to stare at his engineer. But Old Bill looked the same as before. Snakey studied his twitching face for a long while until the engineer continued in a voice that was sunk to a burned-out whisper:

"Snakey, that—that was the Divil callin'. He was callin' me. *Seven days from now—next Friday mornin' at 1:23—he's goin' to come after me!*"

"Bushwah, Bill! Bunk! Baloney! Prune juice!" growled Snakey, lighting another cigarette and staring at Bill with a wilted, half-credulous gaze which belied his words of unbelief.

"It ain't bunk, Snakey," denied the engineer. "I know—I know what you think. That's why I ain't never told nobody about it.

But back in the old country—"

Then for thirty minutes the engineer poured out to the man who was closer to him than a brother, the story of the Devil's call.

"Yuh see, Snakey," he concluded. "I thought I could cross the water an' shake him off my trail. But—but— well, it ain't no use, Snakey. When the Divil calls, yuh got to be goin'. There's no gittin' around it."

Once more the fireman tossed away a half-burned cigarette. Once more he shrugged his sloping shoulders and growled in a voice still more unconvinced than before:

"Bushwah, Bill! Applesauce an' prune juice! When yuh go home this mornin', git some uh the old brand. Git gloriously drunk, sleep it off, an' fergit it."

IV

BUT Bill could not forget it. Even if his conviction had been less firm, the boys would not have permitted, once the story leaked through. Wherever he went it was, "Hey, Bill! Snakey says yuh got a date with the Devil. Lei us in on it, won't yuh?" Or maybe, "Oh, Bill! Better go back to the old kind. I drunk some uh that once."

They never gave him a moment's rest, for the skeptics who had not heard the cry would not believe.

Moreover, when the broad light of day had dissipated the Ozark mists, Old Horseface and Alki and the head shack had little faith in an Irish spook on American soil. To them it was simply "applesauce." They insisted the wail had come from a panther or a catamount, although neither of those beasts had been seen in the Ozarks for years.

At home that morning, as soon as he had gulped down a cup of hot coffee, he turned to Katie with the calm announcement:

"Darlin', I believe I'll go talk to Father O'Brien a few

minutes."

Katie stuck her hands on her hips and stared at him sharply. Bill averted his eyes. He hadn't been to confession for more than ten years.

"Why, Bill, what—Sure, sure, run right on down, Bill. It'll be doin' ye good," she murmured.

Bill blushed like a schoolboy and started down the street. Katie stood looking after him, shaking her head.

"Now wouldn't that beat ye?" she muttered. "I wonder—"

Katie prepared lunch and as soon as her husband returned, they sat down at the kitchen table. While Old Bill was mincing at the delicious fish, Little Bill, who had been firing passenger, came bursting in. His face was ripped from ear to ear in a delighted grin.

"Hi there, dad!" he called gleefully, almost before he had got rid of his tin grip. "Some uh the boys down at the roundhouse jist told me you'd been hearin' things."

Katie glanced quickly at her husband. Bill's trembling hand spilled hot coffee down his shirt front. His son continued in the same bantering tone:

"They said you an' Old Nick's been havin' a confab an' yuh had a date with him fer— Why, mother, what's the—"

The rent in the son's face closed. He sprang quickly to his mother's side, clasped her swaying form, kissed her bloodless lips, looked questioningly down into his father's drawn face.

"What is it, mother?" he questioned.   "Dad, what's wrong?"

"Nothin', son," denied the engineer. "Nothin' more'n you've already been hearin'.   Nothin' you can help with."

Katie struggled from her son's arms and stumbled across to her husband. Dropping upon her knees beside him, she lifted her terrified eyes to his.

"Did — did you hear — it, Bill? Don't tell me you heard the

call."

Bill nodded.

"Wan twintv-three, Katie darlin'. Wan twinty-three Friday mornin'."

"What's one twenty-three Friday mornin', dad?" asked the oldest son. "Why don't you tell me?"

Bill looked mournfully from wife to son, and with a shake of his head spoke sadly.

"Ye can tell 'im, Katie darlin'. Tell 'im if you want to. The boy'll have to know sooner or later. Me? I got to be goin' to work now."

V

Two days later Old Bill was assigned a regular turn in the passenger pool. Though he had looked forward to this promotion for years, it gave him now no feeling of elation. He ate little during the week. He slept less. He was like a condemned murderer who paces his cell knowing that his hour is at hand.

True, at times, there came a glimmer of hope, hope that after all he might have been mistaken in the cry, hope which set his Irish wit to work, combating the despondency within. Surely in a new world there would be a new devil. The old one would have no sway. But then, in this country, they prayed to the same God, through the same priesthood. He hadn't thought of that before.

Then his hopes would lurch off on a new tack. For instance, the old curse had decreed that the son must hear the father's warning. *He* had heard it. Thai's how he knew. But Little Bill had been in Bloomfield that night. His oldest son had not heard the call. Perhaps, after all, the magic spell might now be broken. But, no, it was the same old call.

Then hope arose once more when he recalled that the devil didn't seem to possess so much territory down on the S. & S. as he had in the old country. There it was the Devil's Bog, the Devil's Hill, the Devil's Forest, the Devil's Bay, the Devil's Cliff. As he remembered the scenes of his boyhood, almost everything seemed to belong to the Devil, and if tradition was to be believed, an O'Reardon had died at every spot the Devil claimed.

Now, down on the S. & S., the only piece of property which bore the name of His Satanic Majesty was the Devil's Curve. Ah, there it was again. The Devil's Curve! The very spot whence had come the cry.

And oh, the irony of it! For he, Old Bill Reardon, had christened that curve and assigned it specifically to the horned king that night while he lay under the old 561, watching the fire lick up the wreckage ten yards away from him after he had turned First 32 over on the curve. Why, oh, why, hadn't he been content to let that spot remain just Stacey's Curve?

Ah, indeed, Father O'Brien was right in saying that Satan worked by devious paths to lure a soul to destruction.

Thursday night came. Little Bill was home in Neyberg. Old Bill was in Bloomfield. All that afternoon he walked the streets, going from pool hall to saloon, or dodging in and out among pinochle games like a restless shadow. About five o'clock he choked down a lunch, and on his way to his room, stopped in at the roundhouse to see when he would probably get out on his run.

For ten minutes he studied the board. He stood to get No. 10. His trembling hands sought the time-table in his hip pocket. He shook it open and stood staring down the row of figures and station names. He gulped, leaned against the counter. Cold perspiration stood in heads upon his forehead. *No. 10 would be passing the Devil's Curve at 1:23!*

He tottered from the office, muttering: "The Devil's Curve— 1:23— Friday mornin'."

If for a second there flashed into his brain the thought of "laying off "and thereby cheating Fate, that thought was crushed by the recollection of the words of a hill-billy philosopher with whom he had tamped ties in his early days on the S. & S. down by Macomb. "What is to be will be, son," the white-haired sage had said," and what hain't, cyan't be."

VI

THUS reconciled, he went to bed and slept the first sound sleep for days, slept and dreamed that he was back among the hedge-bordered lanes of Ireland. At 7:30 the call boy came for him, knocking, rapping, pounding on the door.

"Mr. Reardon!" bellowed the youth. "Hey, there, Reardon!"

Bill crawled dazedly from his bed to open the door.

"What yuh got, kid?" he growled as the youngster shoved the call book under his nose.

"Yuh gittin' Second No. 6 at 8:40. Engine 1323," returned the boy. "Don't go back to bed now, dammit."

Signing the book, Bill handed it hack without comment.

"Second 6 at 8:40!" he muttered as the boy closed the door and went down the hall. Hope once more! "Second 6 at 8.40! Why—why, that is only ten minutes late on Six's regular time. And No. 6 is due at Rome at 12:40."

He rubbed his hands together gleefully. Why he, Bill Reardon, would pass the Devil's Curve nearly an hour ahead of time, if nothing happened! He put on clean overalls, jammed down the black cloth cap and adjusted the blue goggles above it. Then, knotting the red bandanna carefully about his neck, he started for the roundhouse.

"To hell with the Divil!" he crooned as he locked the door. "To hell with the Divil an' all his imps."

When he reached the engine, Snakey was already there, had the blower on and black smoke rolling from the stack.

"Hello, Snakey!" he greeted cheerily as he climbed into the cab.

Snakey wriggled about in astonishment. This was the first decent greeting Bill had given him for a week.

"Why—why, howdy, Bill! You goin' out to-night, are yuh?"

"Damn right I'm goin' out, Snakey. Didn't think I'd turn down a chance to make ten dollars, did yuh?"

Snakey shrugged his sloping shoulders, and took a puff at his cigarette. Bill lighted the torch and dropped down with the long-necked can and wrenches to oil around. Ten minutes before leaving time he backed the No. 1323 against the string of Pullmans which the 1345 had just left standing on Track 3. A hundred feet behind him, the 1357 stood coupled to First No. 6, her green signals glowing like-cat eyes.

Down toward the station lights blinked and jostled. A white one rose and fell in a highball. The bell of 1357 clanked, and First No. 6 went panting by him, exactly on time. Five minutes later the air inspector climbed to the engine to make his report.

"Fourteen cars. All working, Reardon."

The inspector was gone and in his place came Conductor Hull with the orders.

"Thought you had a date with the Devil to-night, Bill," laughed the conductor, handing the engineer a single-tissue sheet wrapped in the clearance.

"Git out with yuh, you old hatchet-faced cake-eater," growled Bill, reddening.

With another laugh the conductor was gone. Bill's hand was steady as he unfolded the tissue sheet and read his running order:

"Engine No. 1323 will run as Second No. 6, Bloomfield to Neyberg."

A smile played about the corners of Bill's mouth as he set his reverse over in the corner and started clanking out past the long row of green sentinel lights down the lead. But from the right side of the cab, he could not see the lightning which played low down in the northwest where a storm cloud was rising all black at the border.

As they stormed along through the darkening night, however, killing time at every station for the block of First No. 6, Bill, watching the lightning climb higher and higher, penciling the cloud with the black border, dropped his air of bravado and relapsed into the grip of despondency which had bound him for the past week.

Snakey watched htm nervously, lighting a cigarette, taking a few puffs from it and tossing it out the open window. Bill was thinking of only one thing—to get Second No. 6 into Neyberg on time. He checked his watch at every mile. He flipped his fingers over the brake valve and over the throttle lever.

At every station he approached, he watched the block eagerly, hoping it might hang red and hold him for seconds. For as long as that block remained against him, First No. 6 was less than ten minutes ahead. If only he could stay on the block, he would pass Devil's Curve by 12:50.

When the engine lagged on a hill he became frantic lest he might lose a minute. He *must* not let First No. 6 leave him. And for a hundred miles he did not.

VII

GOING down the grade into Forgan, however, he had to set his brakes to check the speed so he would not have to stop there for the block. When he released them, there came two short blasts from the air whistle.

Now two blasts from the air whistle means, "Stop at once!" For a second, he hesitated. Then, while a tremulous left hand twisted the brake valve, a more tremulous right one groped above for the whistle cord with which to answer the signal.

When Bill looked back, he caught his breath and groaned. Halfway along the train a stream of fire was flying out from the wheels, fire not made by rubbing brake shoes.

"What—what is it, Snakey?" he called anxiously across to the fireman.

"Looks like a brake beam draggin'," answered the fireman disgustedly.

For almost thirty minutes the two men watched eagerly while

the train-men worked disconnecting the dragging beam. Neither mentioned the thing uppermost in their minds, the spook at Devil's Curve, but both of them were praying they would leave Forgan at a time that would not put them at Rome at 1.23. They looked at watches thirty times in less than that many minutes, and they compared for correctness three times during the interval.

Bill climbed down from the cab and paced to and fro. Snakey lay coiled up on his seat box smoking, smoking. Would they never get that brake beam done?

Finally, the conductor's lantern signaled, "Whistle in the flag." With trembling hands Bill clutched the grab irons. With feet which could hardly find the steps he climbed to his cab, stumbled to his seat and, clutching the cord, sent out four long blasts of his whistle.

A minute later the light lifted in high ball, and Bill Reardon dragged Second No. 6 into Forgan thirty-one minutes late. The order board was out here. The fireman picked up the hoop and handed Bill the order. Bill's voice shook as he read aloud:

"Second No. 6, Engine 1323, will meet No. 5, Engine 1311, at Freeland."

Bill gave a sigh of relief. Blood surged once more to his gray, grimy face. The Irish smile, sickly and wan, yet full of hope was on his lips when he handed the sheet to Snakey. If they met No. 5 at Freeland they would not reach Devil's Curve until after 1:23.

Bill slipped back his throttle and went thundering away toward Freeland. By the time he came to the switch, he had made up a minute of his lost time. He whistled for the station, whistled his meet, watched the red eye that marked the order board. It didn't change to green. A white light beneath it highballed — signal that the station had orders for him.

One more Snakey grabbed the hoop and passed him the tissue sheet. This time the fireman did not wait for him to read the order.

The two heads bent together. Two gasps escaped tightening throats, two prayers went to the Almighty. This order read:

"Second No. 6, Engine 1323, will take siding and meet No. 5, Engine 1311, at Rome instead of at Freeland."

For a full minute they stood in the gangway, staring each at the other. Then, dropping into his seat, Old Bill Reardon opened his throttle and Second No. 6 thundered up the grade out of Freeland. Within eight minutes, at 1:23, he would pass the Devil's Curve!

VIII

IN Neyberg, Dispatcher Mason, who issued orders for the movement of east end trains, having cleared No. 5, shoved the phone from him, commenced eating his midnight lunch. At an adjoining table, Smithers, the night chief, was burning up the wires with a batch of west end orders.

Mason hit into a chicken sandwich, hut with the bite still between his teeth, quickly laid it down and grabbed for his order file. His eyes showed white. His hand trembled as he snatched off the top clearance—clearance given to No. 5 .at the passenger station five minutes ago.

Quickly he thumbed through the batch of tissue sheets and checked them with the clearance. His face went gray. He scarcely breathed. He grabbed for the file once more, checked down to the order he had issued Second No. 6 at Forgan.

"God!" he exclaimed.

He brushed the sandwich aside and with a glance at the tense figure of the chief, snatched the phone and plugged in, ringing frantically.

"Hello! Hello, Neyberg!" he croaked. "No. 5 gone?"

"No. 5 out 1:16," came the reply. "Just going—"

Quickly he rang again. He glanced at the clock. It was 1:18.

"Freeland speaking," came over the wire.

"Freeland, is Second 6 gone?"

"Second 6 through at 1:15. Anything wrong?"

Without answering, Mason dropped his headgear and called huskily:

"Take it, Smithers. Fo'r God's sake, take it, and call out the big hooks!"

"What's the matter, Mason?" queried the chief, coining to his side. "What's wrong with you?"

"I pulled an awful boner, Smithers. I put out a meet with 5 and Second 6 at Freeland. Five fell down a bit and I changed the meet to Rome and forgot to give 5 a copy of the order. My God, Smithers! They'll hit," groaned the dispatcher." Nothin' can keep 'em apart—nothin'—an' Old Bill Reardon'll be wheelin' that Second 6 like a bat out uh hell, tryin' to make up lost time. Oh Lord! Do somethin', Smithers! If you don't do somethin' they'll hit square on the Devil's Curve. They're timed exactly right. Nothin' can stop 'em."

"Keep your shirt on. Mason. Don't go gittin' ready for the bughouse till you hear from 'em anyway. Anything can happen in five minutes. Get over there in that chair and don't be a fool."

Within two minutes, Smithers, in anticipation of the catastrophe, had ordered both wreckers *at once*. Had called superintendent, trainmaster and roadmaster, and was clearing the line of freight traffic so that he might get the wrecker outfits through if the two trains got together. This done, he sat at the desk waiting, waiting.

At 1:25 the city telephone rang. The chief grabbed the receiver with nerveless hand and held it to his ear.

"Mr. Smithers speaking," he informed, trying to hold his voice steady … Yes … Oh, Engineer Reardon? Yes. Yes, he's pulling Second No. 6 tonight, Mrs. Reardon … Yes, Second 6 … is Second 6 all right? Why—ah—why, Mrs. Reardon," stammered the chief, "what makes you think there might be something wrong with Second No. 6?"

"My God, Smithers!" groaned the man who had made the blunder. "Does she—"

Smithers signaled for silence. He was speaking again into the telephone.

"Well, Mrs. Reardon, I may as well tell you—the office here made a—ah, made a mistake. We're hoping to get it cleared up without accident, but—"

There was a crazy click in the receiver as if the telephone on the other end had been suddenly upset, or perhaps dropped to the floor. Smithers called central trying to get a reconnection. But the report finally came, "Your party does not seem to answer."

"How'n hell did that old dame know somethin' was wrong with that Second 6, Smithers?" queried Mason through chattering teeth. "Pray tell me how?"

"Reason enough, Mason, reason enough if there's anything in telepathy. Not only is Old Bill Reardon pullin' Second 6 tonight, but Little Bill's firin' No. 5. Smoke that, will yuh? And they're both in hell by this time —unless there's been a miracle!"

IX

WHEN Second No. 6 pulled away from Freeland, Old Bill Reardon sat erect, scarcely breathing. Cold sweat stood on his forehead. His cab windows were open. The wind whizzed through. He squinted close to watch the track.

Sheet lightning flared and blazed up from the north, hung poised, and slid down into the trees on the south. Twin ruts of curving steel glistened and glimmered. When darkness reigned, the headlight plowed on feebly, making ghosts of trees and poles and skeleton snags, ghosts which glared evilly hack at him as he rushed down the winding trench toward the curve where Death and Devil waited.

They were running fast—too fast for the sharp curves of Freeland Hill. The cab lurched until Snakey could scarcely stand as he put in his last fire. He glanced across at Bill. Outwardly the engineer was as calm as on any one of three thousand other nights he had fallen down Freeland Hill.

A crossing post rushed toward them. Reardon reached for the whistle cord and the crossing signal drowned the sound of thunder, the roar of breaking storm. Then he twisted the brake valve to check his speed for the grade two miles above the Curve. He looked at his watch. It was 1:20. He glanced at his speedometer—forty miles an hour.

He kicked off his brakes, let the heavy train roll on. A painted pole gleamed on his right—a mile and a quarter to Devil's Curve. The hand on the brake valve trembled.

Old Bill leaned far out into the night. A flash of lightning brighter, bigger than the rest seemed to rise out of the north. The whole sky burst into flame. Every tree, every snag on the hillside above was nodding, reckoning. Even the towering limestone cliffs seemed reeling with the crash of the thunder which followed.

Old Bill sprang to his feet, uttered one frightened cry, stood trembling, choking. His left hand gripped the brake valve as in a vise.

Snakey writhed down into the deck and up again. As the heavy string of Pullmans twisted down the grade, he stood gripping the window sill, ready to leap headlong from the speeding train.

The hand which clutched the brake valve twitched and jerked. With what remaining will he had, Old Bill Reardon sought to stay it, then to remove it. But it was as if another hand had closed around it. The brake valve moved one tiny bit, then fairly leaped around. Air whirred and hissed. A hundred wheels sloughed fire, and on the Devil's Curve at 1:23 Second No. 6 ground to a stop. Lights played along the ground beside her. Voices called. A lantern swung toward the engine.

Off to the left a cone of light played through the trees. It crept nearer, as No. 5 dragged up the hill. It swung in sight around the curve. With a cry of terror, Snakey hurled himself from the cab window.

There was another grinding of brakes, another sloughing of fire, and No. 5 stopped, her headlight glaring into the windows of 1323. Voices raised in angry argument between the pilots.

"What in hell you fellers doin' out here?" stunned Conductor Hull of Second No. 6. "I got a meet with you at Rome."

"An' I want to know what the hell you fellers doin' out here," came back the engineer of No. 5. "I got a meet with you at Freeland."

The two men compared orders, then stared about them.

"What stopped you fellers out here?" finally asked the engineer, scratching his head.

"Why—why, really, Hawkins, I don't know," returned the conductor. "I was just comin' over to the engine to find out when you fellows showed up."

"Who's the guy pullin' your drag to-night?"

"Old Bill Reardon."

He whistled. There was a quick movement at his elbow, and a startled voice stammered: "Where—where is dad?"

"Why, I don't know, kid," replied the conductor, flashing the lantern into young Bill Reardon's anxious face. "Come to think of it, I ain't seen him since we stopped."

Snakey Thompson, wiping blood from a dozen scratches he had incurred in jumping, came up from outside the right-of-way, and the four men hurried to the cab of 1323.

Old Bill Reardon sat, both hands closed lightly over the brake valve, as if he were asleep. The conductor shook him.

Finally, Bill found his voice.

"Why—why, ain't I dead?"

"Dead! Hell, no, you ain't dead, you old spook chaser! But you would 'ave been, an' so would a lot more of us, if you hadn't been so all fired sure you was goin' to be."

The next day's *Republican* carried a little news item which began as follows:

WRECK MIRACULOUSLY AVERTED

What seems almost a miracle occurred last night when William Reardon, of Neyberg, engineer on Second No. 6, in the act of fainting in his cab twisted his brake lever, thereby bringing his train to a stop in time to avert a head-on collision with No. 5.

Peace flooded Old Bill's soul. The Irish *banshee* had not found its way to the New World, after all!

Vengeance

A story of Rud Randall, engineer

I

March of Progress

IN the late 70's the Southwestern Railway left St. Louis heading for Texas. The survey led down Coon Creek to Green River, and out to the flats through a narrow, green vale called Travis Hollow.

The "Holler" belonged to "Kaintuck" Randall and Jed Travis, a pair of old hill-billies who had come to the Ozarks, discovered it, liked it, laid land warrants on it, and hewn out homes. When company agents approached with question of right-of-way, the old boys backslid, told the agents where to go, and reckoned there wasn't "nobody goin' fer to take our medder land fer to build no hell-damned railroad through."

But personal prejudice did not halt the march of progress. The Southwestern got the land. It offered to pay Jed and Kaintuck a fair sum.

Instead of taking the money and building "plank" houses with it, as their neighbors did, these two obstinate old fellows went to "lawr."

They fought through circuit court, court of appeals, and

supreme court; and when they got out, the railroad had the heart slice of their little farms, slick lawyers had the money for it, and they had sterile strips running up into the rocky hills on each side.

"Robbed" thus of the fruits of their life-time labor, they came to despise the railroad with all the venom of which a hill-billy soul is capable, and to regard it as the personification of hell, sin, and the devil.

So regarding things, and having failed to secure "jestice" in human courts, they appealed their case to a higher tribunal. They began praying for heavenly vengeance, at the same time striving to inoculate the hearts of their fifteen-year-old sons with that bitter hatred which they themselves kept alive by hours of brooding.

In "Gyp" Travis the venom struck home. At fifteen he was cursing the railroad, the men who had built it, the men who ran its trains, vowing: "Some day I'm a-goin' to git even with 'em. I'm a-goin' to make 'em wisht they'd never took my pap's land to build no railroad over."

Rud Randall reacted differently. Despite prayer, admonition, threat and punishment, he would sneak up the hillside, hide in the brush, watch with raptured fascination the brass-bound diamond stacks racing by, and allow that "Some uh these days I'm a-goin' into Wellfield an' git a job as engineerman on one uh them ar monsters."

One evening in September, 1881, two filthy, ragged railroad bums ambled out of the east carrying dirty packs from which blackened tomato cans dangled. When they came to the Travis cabin, they climbed from the cut and shuffled along the right-of-way fence, hunting the entrance to the right-of-way. Failing to find it, one of them laid a hand on the top wire, which ran close to the south chimney, and called:

"Hallooo!"

Two hounds set up a commotion. Old Jed came to the door.

Gyp Travis and Rud Randall slipped out past him. The bum backed away from the nine strands of hog wire with two vicious dogs behind it.

"Mister," he whined, "could youse give a poor devil a little coffee?"

Old Jed hitched his galluses, strode out to the door, and pointed dramatically up the tracks.

"Git!" he bellowed, "Git out!"

"But, mister—"

"Don't mister me! Cit back to yore hell-damned railroad an' keep a-goin'!"

Jed reached for the squirrel rifle under the eaves. The bums rolled into the cut and with fearful backward glances hurried around the curve.

A MILE up the hollow was a long trestle of heavy pine timbers. Above the trestle a big spring came from under a limestone bluff. They went up by the spring, built a fire, cooked a mulligan stew, gathered leaves for a bed and dead branches for a jungle fire, and turned in.

Shortly after dark a freight train came in from the east and doubled[1] over the hill into Glennwood. Without telling the folks where they were going, Gyp and Rud sneaked through the barn-yard and went up to the tracks to see what all the whistling was about. Gyp did not want to go, but Rud and his boyish curiosity overcame his prejudice.

Where the train had stopped, they approached the fence to reconnoiter. A red lantern was on the end of a tie by the head car. Markers burned on the rear. Far down the track a red light and a white one gleamed in the dull glow of the full moon. The train appeared deserted. Presently two stealthy figures came slipping

---

1 "Doubling a hill" designated the practice of cutting a too-heavy train in half and hauling each section up the grade independently.

down the tracks.

"It's them bums," Gyp whispered. "Le's go back home."

"A-a-a, they won't hurt us," said Rud. "Le's stay an' watch."

Slinking from sight, they hid behind a clump of brush close to the right-of-way fence.

One on each side of the train, the bums went to the caboose and came back. They stopped at the door of a box car and began fumbling with the fastener. A seal wire snapped. A bolt clicked. A door eased back.

One bum crawled into the car. The other remained outside, keeping fearful watch. The boys scarcely breathed. Within the car a match flared and burned out, and another and another. The bum reappeared at the door.

"Dey ain't nothin' to eaf in this rattler, Jimmie." Every whispered word carried to the boys' ears. "But dey's plenty to drink. It's a carload uh bottled whishky."

"Whisky?" The whispered exclamation was exultant.

He hushed. From up the hill came five bellows from the steamboat whistle of the old eight-wheeler, calling in the flagman from the east. The bum in the car disappeared. A moment later he was back in the door with a wooden case. He dropped the case to the floor. His partner picked it up and hustled it to the ground. They shoved the door into place, bolted it, slipped the seal wire back, and snatched up their loot.

For ten seconds they looked toward the woods, as if hunting a hiding place. The dump of brush loomed black in the moonlight. They climbed the cut, heading for it.

Even Rud was frightened. He wished himself safely back at the Travis place, where two lean hounds, a squirrel rifle, and a grizzled mountain man would protect him.

The bums came halfway to them, then, as if having just seen the brush pile thirty yards up the fence, changed direction and went stumbling toward it.

The boys breathed easier. They crawled around and worked out of sight. The train pulled away. Carrying their prize through the fence, the bums returned to their camp and proceeded to get drunk.

WHEN they had gone, Gyp grinned at Rud and said, "Phew! That shore was a close call!"

The boys got up and watched the disappearing wanderers.

"What we goin' to do about it?" Rud queried.

"Nothin'." Rud Randall might be the leader of this pair in woodcraft and adventure, but at fifteen Gyp Travis was developing a cynical philosophy of his own. "Car belongs to the railroad, don't it?"

"Sure."

"Bums belongs to the railroad, too. We can't help it if a railroad bum robs a railroad box car."

Rud had to admit they couldn't.

"Well, we've saw all there is to see. Le's go home."

They went. They did not tell Jed Travis where they had been nor what they had seen. If they had, Jed would have "skinned Gyp alive" for hanging around the railroad when he had been told not to, and Kaintuck Randall would have "licked Rud till he couldn't stand up" for the same reason.

After supper, Kaintuck and Mary Randall came across the fields to the Travis place.

Like his obstinate old neighbor, Kaintuck was a stolid six-footer with frost on his long hair and tobacco stains on his unkempt beard. Like Jed's, his features were hard; for hatred, malice, and resentment are hot boomerangs which sear and scar and wither the features and souls of those who use them.

After a brief visit the two families gathered in the front room for evening worship, as they had done for thirty years. They sang a hymn. Jed read from the ancient Book with its silver clasps, and when he had finished reading they all knelt on the home-made carpet.

Long and earnestly he prayed for their souls' regeneration, their bodies' preservation, and their enemies' damnation. Kaintuck punctuated the fervent pleas with "Amens" which grew louder as the petition continued, and Gyp sniggered guardedly and nudged Rud's shoulder.

THE Ozarks are underlaid with limestone. Trickling waters have dissolved and carried away vast quantities of the rock, leaving the region honeycombed with caverns. Once in ages past such a vast cavern had extended for miles beneath the flats to the west. Its weakening roofs had caved in, forming a chain of sink-holes, locally called "breakdowns," with narrow ridges where the roofs had not yet fallen.

Over the ridge between Big Breakdown and China Pig Hole, depressions each a hundred feet deep with unfathomed pools of blue water in their bottoms, the Southwestern had stretched its steel. There was no reason why it should not have done so. The ridge was crowned with solid rock, which apparently reached the earth's very core.

But the first rolling wheel had struck from it a hollow booming sound, as from a bridge of echoing steel. Kaintuck had heard it. To him it had been a revelation. In that rumbling bridge, which beyond doubt spanned some dark vast cavern, his superstitious mind read the promise of answer to a prayer for vengeance.

"Sometime," Kaintuck whispered, "that ridge'll cave in an' send one uh them brimstone-eatin' implements uh Satan straight into the pits uh hell, an' then they'll have to take their railroad some'eres else."

The idea thus conceived became an obsession. Unaware that those rash prayers were influencing youthful souls, little dream-

*The hill-billies lived and prayed
for vengeance ...*

ing how the fate of their sons was to be bound up in the inescapable answer, they lived and hoped and prayed for vengeance.

The bums stayed on at the spring. They also stayed drunk. The Travis family never saw them; but an old "dominecker" rooster and two hens disappeared; and sometimes when the wind was right, odor of smoke and sound of drunken singing was wafted through the wooded hollow.

The October sun slid down a mackerel sky. Coughs of wind sent flocks of leaves scurrying along the bottom wires of the right-of-way. Rud and Gyp ground the chopping ax at the home-made stone in the chimney corner.

When it was sharp, they chopped wood, milked the cows, fed the pigs. Then they ate supper by candlelight, and having filched precious matches from the family store, started for the "Breakdowns."

The dark night was right for possum hunting. Not a gleam in earth or sky. Soft wind sobbed through skeleton trees, and tick-tacking lonely leaves still clung to deserted branches. Hounds at heel, the boys trudged toward the big trestle, under which they always crossed the tracks to the south side. They stopped. The hounds lifted their heads, sniffed, yawned.

"Nothin' but a cotton-tail," Rud muttered.

Gyp puckered his lips and whistled. Then he hummed:

Watch out, backslidah, whah yo' walkin'

'Spects de Debbil's trompin' around.

Fust yo' know he'll tell yo' howdy

Lift his hoof an' stomp—

Suddenly he stopped. As they rounded the last curve below the trestle, they caught the gleam of firelight on the trees. The dogs commenced growling.

"It's jist them bums up there at the spring."

"I don't—you don't reckon they'd—"

"Naa-a-a! They won't hurt us. They're harmless as a coupla ol' tomcats with their tails tied together."

THE boys walked on. Soon they saw the fire was not at the spring. The bums had moved camp down under the trestle. With the growling dogs at heel, the boys came within the circle of light. The bums raised their weary limbs from their leafy couch and eyed them suspiciously.

"Ain't youse de kids from down where de wild man lives?" one asked drunkenly.

"Yessir." Rud chuckled. He remembered how Old Jed Travis had reached for the squirrel rifle when they had come by.

The burn was on his feet now. His red-rimmed eyes were glowing, and he was pointing up the hollow.

"Well, git a-goin' then!" he barked.

Gyp moved, but Rud didn't.

"Did youse hear me!" The bum took a step toward him. "Dis is *our* hell-damned railroad. You—"

He reached for a dirty pack. The boys did not wait to see what he had in it. Fifty yards away they stopped to look back.

"Did yuh see how close that fire was to them bridge timbers?" Rud asked.

"Ain't our fire," philosophized Gyp, "nor our bridge timbers."

Rud did not argue. The light blinked out behind a turn in the trail. The hounds struck into the deep woods and the hunt was on.

Clouds thickened. Fog spread over the hills. By midnight the boys had forgotten bums and railroad and had gathered six "big 'uns" off limbs where the dogs had treed them. Despite paternal command never to "go nigh that sin-infestered railroad," they were trudging homeward down the tracks.

Near the big trestle Gyp stopped.

"We'd better crawl over the fence and go through the woods," he said.

Rud recalled how ignominiously they had retreated from the hobo camp. He answered, "They wouldn't hurt us none."

As they advanced the fog brightened. A crimson tint came on it, as if blood-mist were clinging to the valley. They stopped, puzzled.

"What is it?" whispered Gyp.

"Them bums has shore got one helluva fire down there," Rud murmured.

"Le's go back a ways an' cut for home."

"Wait a minute." Rud laid a detaining hand on his companion's sleeve. "Le's sneak down a little farther an' see."

Reluctantly Gyp followed. The crimson tinge deepened. To right and left they could see the outline of steel rails, with the embankment falling away. Soon they heard a sullen roar. They sniffed the air. The odor of pine smoke was in it.

"Le's go back home!" There was a tremor in Gyp's voice.

"Nope. We're goin' down there an' see. Maybe them fellers has let that bridge git afire."

"Won't hurt us none if they have." A moment of silence. "Besides, they're liable to kill us."

"We got a good choppin' ax, ain't we?"

RUD laid three dead possums in the middle of the track and moved forward, gripping the ax handle. Excitement gleamed in their eyes as the memory of the drunken bums dimmed. They quickened their steps, broke into a run, and came to the western end of the trestle.

Eighty feet long and thirty feet high, the structure was braced with heavy pine timbers. From its full length flames were licking the murky sky. Open-mouthed, the boys watched. A crack like a gunshot rang on the midnight air. They both jumped. Gyp grabbed Rud's sleeve,

"What's that?" he asked hoarsely.

"Hot sandrock bustin'."

Rud's tone was not exactly convincing. He remembered those two bums vividly. Gripping the ax, he turned, intending to go on home. He took three steps. Another idea flashed into his brain.

The Midnight Express! It was due. Night after night he had lain awake listening to the roar of its exhaust, to the whistle screaming through the darkness as the engineer raced across the valley for the hill beyond.

He dropped the ax and grabbed Gyp's shoulder.

"We—we got to go back," he said thickly.

"Back where?"

"Back up there an stop that midnight train. She'll be comin' down the hilt any minute. If she's battin' along like she usually is, there'll be a terrible wreck."

"Let it. Railroad train, railroad bridge."

"But the people! There's passengers. And there's an—an engineerman."

"Well, I ain't a goin' back. Them bums might be up there an' kill us."

"All right. Go on home. I don't aim to let a lot of people be killed."

Rud scarcely knew what he was saying. His nervous fingers jerked from Gyp the bundle of pine slivers they had been using for a torch, divided it, gave Gyp half of it. Then he struck out up the track.

At forty yards his light failed. On and on he held to his stumbling run. He did not know how far he had come or how far he should go.

He was stumbling over another trestle. His right foot missed the tie. He pitched into the track, lay there for a moment, chewing gravel. When he came up, there was a roaring in his ears like a rush of waters.

Was that the Express? He listened. His head cleared. No, it was only the wind. He wiped blood from his cut lip and struggled on.

When he could run no farther, he slowed to a walk. He thought he must be near the Big Breakdown. He listened for the sound of the whistle. There was no sound.

He began to think. Misgivings came. What if those bums should set upon Gyp going alone down that dark hollow. It was a terrifying thought.

What if something had happened to the Express? What if the one o'clock going west should come first tonight, as it had once last week? It would come tearing up from the east and plunge through that chasm where the bridge used to be! Why had he not thought of that sooner?

A minute passed. He was scared. He fingered the matches in his pocket, plucked a blackened sliver from his pitch torch. He remembered the tune Gyp had been singing:

Watch out, backslidah, whah yo' walkin'

From behind him a cry was rising on the night. It started a low wail, rose to a piercing shriek, and ended in an agonized moan. He caught his breath. Then he laughed nervously. It was only a panther.

HUMMING the tune, he moved restlessly forward. The fog had thinned. He could see the contour of the land. He was at the east end of the ridge separating China Pig Hole from Big Breakdown. He remembered the prayer his Pap and Uncle Jed had been praying. He shivered. Maybe that prayer had been answered.

He moved toward the west end of the ridge. Foot upraised, he stopped, gasped, and looked back and forward. From somewhere ahead, visible through the thinning fog, he caught the glow of light. It came from the dank floor of the Big Breakdown, rising slowly, hanging in midair like a ghostly spirit. It brightened, rose, dimmed to a dull phosphorescent glow, and faded.

He stood upon the narrow ridge watching for it to return. The Express whistled away in the west. Rud did not hear it. It whistled again, and a dull hum came into the night. Rud did not move. He was afraid.

Then from the darkness behind came once more that blood-curdling panther cry. Rud started, then plunged forward. Racing to make up lost time, the Express careened through the cut beyond the ridge. Its whistle screamed, and its headlight dashed the fog. It had come unseen upon him.

He reached for his matches. He grabbed for the slivers of pitch. But it was too late now. He was in the middle of the track. Snatching off his cap, he waved it wildly, frantically. The whistle shrieked a warning.

Not until the pilot was within twenty feet of him did he fling his cap and leap toward the left, toward Big Breakdown. He crashed through briars and brush and rolled into the barbed wire fence sixty feet below.

Rud's first stunned thought was that the train had gone on, that it would plunge into the burning bridge. His second was that he was left alone here where ghost lights glowed, and wild beasts waited. His third was that he was bound hand and foot, and ten thousand needles were prodding weary flesh. He groaned and quit thinking for awhile.

Far away, very far away, men were talking and feet were walking. Light broke through the fog.

"It was about here," a heavy voice boomed. "He was right square in the middle of the track, an' my pilot almost hit him,"

"Hit hell!" scoffed another. "You never even saw anything, much less hit it."

"I tell you I did. Looked like a kid, an' I think he was tryin' to flag me."

There was scornful laughter.

"You never saw a cockeyed thing, Jim. You been hearin' so much about them two old devils down Travis Holler praying for this ridge to cave in that—"

The laughter drifted away. Rud was trying to get loose. He regained consciousness sufficiently to know that he was not tied, that he was tangled up in a hog wire fence.

While he struggled the lights and voices went to the west end of the ridge and returned. Men were still arguing.

"I tell you, Jim, you was asleep when you hit this ridge."

"You've been drinking the wrong brand, Jim."

"An' I tell you I wasn't dreamin', an' I've not drunk a drop since pay day."

Rud tried to call to them. He was terrified when no sound

came. His lips were dry. He licked them and tried again. A hoarse shout split the night.

"Here! Here! Down in the fence!"

THE men stopped. For what seemed hours they peered into the darkness. Then a black man and two white ones in uniform and a giant in overalls stumbled down the embankment to disentangle him from barbed wire.

"Hurt?" was Jim Weatherby's first question.

"No. No, I ain't hurt."

"What'n hell was you doin' out there in that track?"

Rud had to think a minute. Finally he remembered.

"The bridge. The bridge over Travis Holler. Some drunk bums burnt it, an' I come back to tell you."

"Bridge over Travis Holler! The hell they did! Why, it's almost four miles to that bridge."

"Yessir, but I thought—I was afraid—"

Rud felt somehow they did not believe him. The conductor raised his lantern.

"Say, ain't you one of them Travis Holler kids?"

Rud flushed. He remembered what he had heard them saying about the "two old devils praying." He raised his aching head and met the stare.

"Yessir, I'm Rud Randall."

"Rud Randall, eh?" The conductor winked at Weatherby. "Right sure you didn't set fire to that bridge yourself?"

Rud was hurt and scared. He had struggled bravely to keep back the tears. At this unkind thrust he commenced to blubber.

"I didn't do no such a danged thing!" he cried hotly.

"Course you didn't, son." The engineer laid a fatherly hand on his aching shoulder and spoke sharply to the conductor.

"You ought to be ashamed of yourself, Chick. Reckon a kid like him would pull a stunt like that an' then risk his neck trying to flag us?"

"How'd he know it was on fire, then?"

Briefly Rud explained about the possum hunt, and the drunken bums, and the fire under the bridge, and their return home.

He did not mention the panther cry, nor the light he had seen coming from the swampy sink-hole. Neither did he mention the matches nor the pitch slivers nor tell them how terrified he had been a few seconds before the train came.

They returned to the train—all except the flagman. The porter cut off the engine. Big Jim took Rud into the cab. The conductor followed, and they eased down the hill to investigate.

Big Jim was the soul of kindness. He kept patting Rud on the knee, and saying: "You're the brave lad. Walk four miles to flag us. Believe me, kid, if you hadn't, there'd sure 'a' been a choice lot of funerals."

They talked about the engine. Rud said he wanted to be "a engineerman sometime." Big Jim did not laugh. Maybe he remembered when he had expressed the same thing in almost the same words. He showed Rud the throttle, the reverse lever, and the gages. The boy watched in fascination.

But his paradise was short lived. The engine came to the bridge, and Big Jim helped him out of the cab. They all went to the west end of the smoldering structure. Rud stood proudly beside the engineer and pointed out the spot where the bums had had their fire.

Gyp had been home. He and Jed and Kaintuck were in the hollow watching the fire. Weatherby walked down the dump and spoke to them. They were not talkative. Kaintuck took Rud by the arm and said sharply: "Le's go home. You ort to have been in bed two hours ago."

THE next morning Kaintuck gave Rud a "genuwine good lickin'" before they went to church. Not for flagging the train and saving a lot of human lives. That was all right! The lickin' was for "disobeyin' a fatherly command and goin' nigh the sin-in-festered railroad."

Sullenly, stubbornly, Rud submitted to the lash. It was not the first nor hardest "lickin'" he had got since the railroad came. He got that the time he rode the side of a box car up to the top of the hill and jumped off, and his father saw him.

During the early morning men came to repair the burned trestle. Around 9.30 a special came from Sayer. The superintendent's private car was on the rear. Rud saw it come while he was hitching up to go to church.

The Travis family came home with them to dinner that day. The women fussed over Rud and tied up his worst cuts and put salve on them. The men did not say much about him.

While they were eating dinner two men in plug hats came swinging up the wagon road from the crossing. The hounds spotted them and set up a commotion. The diners craned their necks, and Rud's pulse quickened. Despite the plug hat, he recognized the tall one as Jim Weatherby.

In answer to their knock, Kaintuck went to the door.

He said, "Howdy!" There was no welcome in the sullen voice. A moment of strained silence, and Superintendent Bain threw away half of a two-bit cigar and met the burning eyes of the farmer.

"Is this where Mr. Randall lives?" he asked.

"I'm Kaintuck Randall!"

"Oh! Well, I'm Bain, superintendent of the railroad here. I wanted to see your son, Rud, please."

"Rud's eatin' his dinner. I'm his pap. You can talk to me."

Rud shoved back his chair. He brushed past his father and stood on the sandstone step facing the railroaders. Kaintuck's jaw went down. He reached out a hand to draw the boy back, then dropped it.

"What is it, sir?" asked Rud.

Bain extended a heavy hand.

"So you're the boy that stopped our train for us last night and kept it from going into the bridge?"

"Yes, sir." Rud was flushing proudly.

"Now that's fine. I'm glad to know boys like you." He looked at Kaintuck. "You ought to be proud of this son of yours, sir," he said.

Kaintuck merely grunted. The others had stopped eating. The super talked to Rud again.

"I came over, Rud, to tell you how much we appreciate your action last night. You probably saved a hundred lives." He fumbled in his breast pocket, found an envelope bearing the trade-mark of the Southwestern. "Here's a trifling token for you. I trust something more substantial may be forthcoming. In this envelope is a wire from our general manager, and a pass for you, and your father and mother."

"A pass!" Kaintuck exclaimed.

"Yes, a pass. A ticket. We thought you might like to ride our trains, and this will let you do so without cost."

Rud's eyes were gleaming. Kaintuck reached over his shoulder and took the envelope. He did not open it.

"We don't need no pass, mister," he said coldly. "We don't want to ride your hell-fired trains, an' don't want no son of mine—"

"But, Mr. Randall—"

Kaintuck was quivering all over. He stepped down beside his son, and, clutching the crumpled envelope in his hand, pointed toward the road.

"There's the path," he quavered. "Take it. You robbed me of my land, now you want to wheedle my boy away from me an' corrupt him, an' send his soul to perdition. You cain't. Now, go!

II

The Devil Had Nothing on Him!

RUD ran away from home that night. He rode a freight into Wellville and hunted up Big Jim Weatherby. Jim was not surprised. Though he knew that very shortly Kaintuck Randall would come seeking a missing son, he took Rud home with him.

Rud stayed at Weatherby's ten days. He met Jim's Molly. She was a lady of thirteen. Because he had kept her father from dying at Travis Hollow, she showed Rud the town; and despite his countryfied ways, treated him like a prince.

Jim urged him to return home. Rud refused. Seeing the futility of argument, Jim loaned him money and squared him out West. Rud's heart went into his brogans when leaving time came. He held Molly's hand, looked into her eyes, and got her promise to write.

He went to Tucson, added years to his age and got a job in the S. P. roundhouse building fires. Soon he was firing on the road, and by the time he was twenty he was running an engine.

Always the Ozarks called, called him to come home. There

was his mother. He wrote her often. She never answered. lie wrote Molly once a month for five years. When he was promoted, he asked her to marry him as soon as he had saved a thousand dollars. After that they wrote more often.

Kaintuck grieved bitterly. He had loved this son of his, loved him with all the soul of an old man who must have something to cling to. He cursed the railroad anew, he prayed with redoubled fervor that the "enemy might be made to suffer. Fires of hatred rapidly gnawed out the wick of life in him. Palsy came, and paralysis; and when Rud had been gone three years, Old Kaintuck, his shriveled soul still crying for vengeance, went to its maker. And in the moment he lay dying, a long freight stormed through the Breakdowns, rumbled over the ridge, sending out its hollow booming echo, as if the Avenger were assuring the Faithful One that a covenant still held.

Gyp remained on the farm. Life grew constantly harder. With the rich meadow land out of tillage, he and his father could scarcely eke a living from the remaining rind. While Rud had been at home, the two boys had been constantly together, hunting, fishing, sleeping, eating. Rud's level-headed-ness had promptly held in such vengeful impulses as Gyp conceived.

Now those impulses had no check. Gyp pictured himself helping "The Almighty" to pour out the vials of his wrath. A burned bridge—a loosened rail—a pile of ties on the curve.

Before he acted, his mind conceived more practical ideas. Instead of mere vengeance, why not collect damages? He remembered two bums stealing whisky out of a box car. It had looked easy. It would be easy!

As if to crystallize his impulse, the summer he was seventeen the Southwestern put a passing track through the meadow just below the house. Never a night or day but trains of freight cars took siding there and remained at least for a few minutes, and sometimes for hours.

IT was in December that he made his first effort to "collect," as he called it. He had always slept in the "loft" reached by an outside stairway. Tonight, instead of going to bed, he went to the barn and waited. About 11.30, No. 55, the westbound merchandise train, whistled for Travis Hollow. Gyp had learned enough of whistle signals to know it was heading in for the Midnight Express. He sneaked away from the barn and caught a box car.

Instead of pulling *through* the siding, freight trains using Travis Hollow always *backed out,* in order to get a run for the hill. Because they did this, the head brakeman remained at the switch and "looked 'em over" as the cars ran by; and trainmen seldom went forward.

Tonight, as Gyp had reckoned, No. 55 pulled into clear and stopped. lie waited a few minutes. No one came from the caboose.

He had no way of knowing, of course, which cars contained usable merchandise, he did not even know that cards show contents, and he would not have dared strike matches to look at them had he known. Consequently, the only thing to do was to open car after car until he found something.

When he reached up to twist off his first seal, the cold hand of fear grabbed him. Before him flashed a vision—barred cells, and armed guards in the foreground. He drove the vision away. He was doing no wrong. He was only collecting—collecting a debt on which payment had been refused. The Devil had nothing on him!

He slipped the broken seal into his pocket—he remembered the bums had done that—slid back the door, and crawled in.

Striking a match, he peered about. The car was loaded with farm machinery. With a snort of disgust, he backed out, closed the door, and threaded the seal wire through the eye.

The next one he tried was loaded with barreled lime. The next with loose wheat, and all seven of them contained not a single thing he could use. He was disappointed.

The next night No. 55 stayed at Glennwood for the Express. The second night it went to Rover. The third it headed in at Travis Hollow.

Gyp was waiting. He rode it into clear. The very first car he opened was loaded with dry goods. He knew it was dry goods because he had seen merchants at Glennwood unpacking boxes like them.

"Now's the time," he whispered.

But it wasn't. To open those cases required a bar or hammer. He had neither. Cursing himself for a fool, hbe shut the door and returned home.

THE next day he went into the shop and made a short wrecking bar, one he could carry in a pocket and conceal in a crack in the barn. When No. 55 stopped again, he was ready. It was a murky night two days before Christmas. He had become bolder now. He set quietly to work.

The third car he opened looked good. There were shoes, piece goods, and underwear. He was in there fifteen minutes. When he came out, he had fifty dollars' worth of merchandise. He took it up the hollow, hid it under a bluff and went home to bed.

The following morning he set out squirrel hunting. He came bounding in an hour later, both arms filled with packages.

"Look, Pap!" he cried. "Look what I found!"

"Where in hell did you find it?"

"Up the holler under a bluff. Maybe bums stole it off the railroad an' put it there intendin' to come back for it."

Jed Travis was credulous. He never questioned his son's veracity, even though every pair of shoes and every suit of underwear fitted some member of the family.

For two years Gyp kept "finding" things up the hollow. Some-times they were under one bluff, sometimes under another, sometimes in a hollow tree. Part of the stuff they used, more of it they sold to the neighbors at "less than cost." Old Jed kept marveling at his son's luck. He could not understand it.

"Maybe, Pap," Gyp suggested piously, "it's the Lord's way of answerin' prayer. Maybe He's took that way of makin' the Southwestern pay back what they robbed you of when they took your bottom medder to build a railroad on."

That explained everything. Jed had prayed, and his prayer had been answered. He offered thanksgiving and asked for "furder blessin's."

When Rud had been gone four years, Jed Travis went up the church hill in a farm wagon and never came back. Gyp and his mother built a little plank house on the knoll and tore down the log one.

With cash, swagger, and good looks, Gyp broke into Glennwood social life. He found more stuff and sold it. The railroad company missed it. They set two railroad bulls to find out where it was going. Three months after his father had gone Gyp stumbled squarely into their arms ten seconds before he was ready to pull the seal off a merchandise car, and only blind luck and quick thinking kept him from being arrested and sent to prison.

A week after this escape he proved his spark of genius. Realizing he would dare "collect" no more off the Southwestern at Travis Hollow, he went to Wellfield and took a job braking. Not that he wanted to work for the railroad. He didn't.

His one mania was to steal from it, to get even with it, and he thought working for them was the easiest way to do it. He expected within a few years to quit and go into the store business, and he even built a shack in Travis Hollow and set his brother up with a handful of merchandise.

Immediately he found that with access to bills of lading, with the freedom of the train, and with a store at Travis Hollow, he could steal the company "blind." Thus he not only wreaked upon the hated Southwestern a vengeance far beyond the fondest dreams of his dead father, but also gained that wealth and power which all men crave. He worked on.

BEFORE he realized it, the spirit of the railroad had hold of him. The Southwestern was a fast pike. Any railroad running over a succession of short, steep grades with intervening valleys is fast, because men must race down grades and across valleys to run the hills beyond. Then, too, they hauled fast stuff—oranges, bananas, fresh meat.

Something in the eternal race with Time and Death, in the odor of grease and the scream of flanges, gripped him as it grips all men who follow it. Even while his one self was hating the company for which he worked and stealing everything he could get his hands on, the other held him to his railroad duty.

He hit the ground running. He flagged long and quickly. He risked his neck to hold trains with hand brakes when the night was cold and the rails were slick. Within a year he had become one of the best brakemen, and within four years one of the best conductors on the job.

He did not take praise seriously. He scoffed and sneered— until he met Molly Weatherby. She became the last powerful magnet which held him to the rails. From the day he knew her he determined that he, not Rud Randall, should lead her to the altar.

When Rud was twenty-two, he came home with a thousand dollars. He first went to Travis Hollow. His eldest sister was living on the home place. She looked him over, kissed him, told him how the old folks had gone, one of them asking for him, the other cursing the Southwestern. She also told him Gyp Travis had gone to work for the railroad, that Gyp was getting rich, and that the company was *paying him* the old account.

Rud was puzzled. He knew it was not like a railroad to go

back of a court decision and pay a debt already settled. He was suspicious, because he not only knew Gyp Travis, but knew why box cars have seals and bulls ride merchandise trains.

He went to Wellfield. He had not written Molly he was coming and wanted to surprise her. He did. When he went to the house at 8.oo P.M., she was in the parlor. The blinds were down and the light was low and Gyp Travis was with her.

The two men shook hands and looked each other over. Rud was a strapping six-footer with a slight stoop to his broad shoulders. He was not exactly handsome, but his face was no mask, and his smile was not fawning.

Gyp was five feet nine and a trifle stout for twenty-two. His black hair was slicked away from a high forehead. Emblems of fraternal orders glistened on his neatly tailored coat. The darkly handsome face wore the smug smile of one who has never known defeat.

Rud felt a trifle awed when, after a brief visit recalling possum hunts, and perch fishing, Gyp went away. He was disappointed when Molly let him take his betrothal kiss. Somehow it was not the kind he had expected. She did not offer him his diamond, but she would not set the day.

She pleaded, "Not now, Rud. Let's wait a little while. We hardly know each other."

Rud waited. While he waited, he got a job running an engine on the Southwestern. Superintendent Bain was glad to have him.

III

A Payment on Account

TIME dispels bitter memories and softens sweet ones. Seven years in the Southwest obliterated from Rud's conscious thinking all recollection of that old paternal hatred, that old prayer for vengeance.

His first trip was on the Alabama meat train. He was doing fifty-five when he crossed the flats. Approaching Big Breakdown, he remembered the night he had flagged Jim Weatherby and heard a panther and seen the will-o'-the-wisp. He smiled grimly.

His pilot wheels struck the ridge. The hollow echo boomed through the midnight stillness. Subconscious memory flashed the old hatred and petition into his mind. He laughed harshly.

The laugh died; the smile faded. His father was gone; Uncle Jed was gone—both gone to test the unknown to which they had prayed. The smile came back, softened now, and indulgent. They were gone; yet the earth had not opened and swallowed the Southwestern. This ridge stood just as firm, just as strong as on the day the first wheel had rolled over it. Smiling dreamily, Rud roared on through the night, every car wheel striking from the ridge that old dull thunder.

Rud was with Molly every time he was in Wellfield. He held her hands and looked into her blue eyes and courted her. But, when he was not there Gyp Travis came and took her riding through the country.

In October Gyp took Rud for a drive. He showed off the speedy sorrels and the shining buggy with its leather upholstery. He drove past a store marked "Travis Brothers," past sonic vacant lots, and stopped before a big house in the residential section.

"All mine!" Gyp boasted. "Every bit of it belongs to your old pal, Gyp Travis."

"Does it?" Rud eyed him keenly, very keenly.

"And how!" Gyp seemed to enjoy his companion's amazement.

"Must have been saving your money."

"Yep. And *making* it."

"Heard the company had been paying on the right-of-way account."

"Yep. The Southwestern decided to settle up." Gyp flicked the whip over a sorrel flank, and a look of uneasiness flashed into his face. "Where did you hear that?"

Rud chuckled. "Little bird told me. Wish they'd pay off the Randall family while they're at it."

"They *might* do it, Rud," Gyp drawled, "if you want to go after it."

"That depends."

"It's a secret formula, old pal."

Gyp turned the team into a woods road and stopped far away from the nearest house. "It's a secret formula," he repeated, "but if you're really interested—"

"I'm not."

"O.K., Rud. Faint heart—you know the rest of it."

Rud knew the rest of it. Gyp drove in silence back to Wellfield.

RUD had a date with Molly that evening. The sorrels were at the gate when he called for her, and he met Gyp coming down the steps. Gyp made a few wisecracks, got into the buggy and drove away.

When Rud went in, he found Jim Weatherby on the war path. Molly was crying. At his approach she fled upstairs, and Jim began raving.

"I wish that sneerin' thievin' so-an'-so would stay away from this house an' let my girl alone."

"What's the matter?"

"Do you mean to stand there an' tell me you don't know what's the matter?"

"Nope. Gyp seems prosperous enough for a conductor."

"Any of us could be prosperous if we'd stoop to do what he's doin'. Randall, are you so dumb you don't know?"

"Nope. Don't *know* anything."

Jim studied for a few minutes. "I don't *know* anything, either," he said slowly, "but I know plenty of men who wouldn't need two guesses. The damned skunk's got every honest railroader on this job under suspicion as a box car thief."

"Ain't anybody slick enough to catch him?"

"Yes. There's plenty of men good enough to catch him. But he's slicker than they. Before he started out, he put soap on his tail; they can't hold him."

Rud did not ask for an explanation. The older engineer stared out across his front yard where the maple leaves were falling. He came close to Rud and laid a hand on a coat sleeve.

"Boy," he said earnestly, "can't you do something? I know why you come back here. Can't you talk that girl into—"

"I've talked to her, Mr. Weatherby," Rud answered slowly. "But you know you can't rush a woman."

Jim nodded.

Molly came downstairs. Her blond hair was fluffed. Her full face was beaming. She gave her father's cheek a playful pinch. She let Rud kiss her.

They went to the opera house, to the play. Rud was thrilled. So was Molly. They sat close together. Rud knew she was drawn to him. At parting that night he held her in his arms, with the autumn moon glinting through the vines on the *front* porch.

"I love you, Molly," Rud whispered.

"Maybe—maybe I love you!"

Rud was happy. An hour afterward he could have kicked himself for not pressing her to name the date. She might have done so and settled everything. But the hour had passed.

RUD did not see Gyp again until the middle of November. They were called for 10.30 P.M. to take a southbound extra. Gyp came to the engine soon after Rud had coupled on. Instead of the smug, masterful Gyp who had driven the spanking team of sorrels down the woods road, Travis was now a businesslike freight conductor.

"We're stuck here for a while," he informed Rud. "They're holding us for a car of stock off the Kansas City Branch."

They sat down on the main line rail. Gyp played with his nickeled lantern, swinging it in a tiny circle between his feet, watching the flash of a big diamond and the play of light on lodge emblems.

They recalled old times together on the farm.

"Gyp, do you remember the time I took the cramps when we were swimmm' in the Bluff hole an' you come in an' got me?"

"Yeah. You remember the time Bailey's bull got me cornered in the woods pasture, an' you come with a pitchfork?"

The brakeman and the fireman listened. They had not known that Gyp Travis and the new "Espee" engineer had known each other.

Around 11:10 the branch line freight came in. A switch engine brought a car of horses and stuck it on the head end. Rud recoupled. When Gyp came with orders Randall was looking at the horses while his five cars of air were pumping up. The conductor stood beside him. The horses were blooded stuff, going home from the State Fair.

"Gosh, but there's some beauts in that bunch," Gyp said admiringly. He had ceased to be the business-like freight conductor now. In his eyes was the gleam of the avenger, and behind it covetousness.

The train line was charged. They were waiting now for No. 52 to pull in from the east. The engineer and conductor leaned against the car.

About the time No. 52 showed the yardmaster came toward them. He was carrying a paper and a pencil. His blue eyes looked as if he had been peering into thick smoke.

"Would you boys like to help us out a little?" he queried.

"Who's grandmother's gone to the poorhouse now?" flashed Gyp.

The yardmaster did not kid back. "It's the night caller, Pat Nilligan."

"What's happened to Pat?"

"Jumped off Fifty-five coming into the yards and ran into the blind end of a string of empties drifting down Track Twelve."

"The devil he did?" There was awe in Gyp's broken voice. "Why, it's not been two hours since that kid called me. He was jokin'."

"We're taking up money to embalm and send the body home to his mother."

Gyp fished a twenty off a roll and handed it to the yardmaster. "If you need more, tell me. Fellow never knows. Yuh might be takin' up a collection to buy me a wooden leg tomorrow."

The yardmaster thanked him profusely. "We can depend on Travis," he said to Rud. "He always throws in *plenty*."

Rud found some silver and passed it over. The yardmaster was gone.

NO. 52 stopped for the long track switch and crawled in. Rud eyed his old pal curiously. The conductor shrugged, looked at the watch.

"The almighty dollar," he apologized, "covers a hell of a lot of sins—even when the railroad furnishes it."

Then he went whistling toward the rear.

They headed in at Ludwig to meet No. 56. Gyp came over the top of the train. While it was running into the siding, he stood on the front end of the horse car, looking down as if something were wrong with it. When they had cleared he cut the air, pulled the pin and signaled ahead.

Rud wondered why he was setting out that car of horses. But he wasn't setting it out. He shoved it into the house track, came against his train, caught some other cars, put the horse car in *behind* them, and recoupled. When he had finished, he walked to the engine.

"There's a weak drawbar on that car they throwed in on us at Wellfield," he explained. "Wonder to me it hadn't pulled out and ditched us."

"Cut it in against the caboose?"

"No. I put it back of these nine heavy loads. It ought to run there all right."

Rud did not think much about the shift. Trainmen often take cars out of the head end of a train and set them farther back to avoid accident and delay.

They left Ludwig forty minutes ahead of the Midnight Express and made good time to Glennwood, being thirty minutes ahead of it there. They had time to make Rover, twelve miles east.

Running through the sag east of Glennwood, Rud saw a light coming over the top of the train. He thought it was the brakeman looking for a hot box.

As they started across the flats toward the Breakdowns, Gyp slid down into the deck.

"We'll head it at Travis Hollow for the varnish," he said quietly.

Rud looked at his watch and at his timecard.

"Why so?" he queried. "We've got time to go up the hill ahead of 'em."

"That damn drawbar on that car of horses don't look too good. I don't want to start up there. I hate to take unnecessary chances on layin' out these fast trains. I served ten days for it once. We'll stay at Travis."

Rud stared up at the conductor. Gyp was looking over Rud's head, where the track curves toward the ridge over Big Breakdown.

Rud said, "You're the brains."

Gyp answered, "Correct, hogger."

He rode the cab down the hill. When they slowed for the switch, he talked to the head brakeman.

"You can drop back to the caboose an' help Garver fix us a bite to eat," he instructed. "I'm hungry as hell." Gyp started out, but turned back to the brakeman.

"Stop the caboose just clear of the peg," he instructed, "so if Fifty-five comes down they'll have room to back in on us."

That was reasonable. The brakeman understood it, and so did Rud.

TRAVIS HOLLOW depot was built with a long high platform behind it. The passing track ran alongside.

Gyp dropped off at the depot and went toward the store. The store was dark, but a moment later a light came on. Seeing the light, Rud reckoned the conductor had aroused his brother Ed to visit while they waited. Very shortly he saw the lantern come out of the store, cross the road to the depot, and go up the high platform.

He oiled around, snuffed his torch and went down the dark side of the train. Nearing the depot, he heard Gyp say guardedly: "They sure are beauts, Ed. They'll make the finest buggy team in this whole country."

A horse snorted. Hoofs struck wood. Rud came even with the car. On the other side were two men with a lantern. Rud saw instantly what had happened. When Gyp had changed that horse car, because of its "weak draw-bar," he had placed it so that when the caboose just cleared the peg it would be spotted at the high platform. The door was open, and Gyp and Ed Travis were taking out two black fillies.

Rud was shocked. Though he had been certain Gyp was stealing, he had never heard of a thief bold enough to steal livestock out of a car at a station platform. One who would do that trick

had not gone a long way on the slippery road. His first thought
was to return to the engine and keep his mouth shut. He reasoned
that sooner or later railroad bulls would catch Gyp and send him
to prison.

Then he recalled the days they had roamed these woods
together. He remembered the vengeful atmosphere which had
surrounded them, remembered how Gyp had responded to it.

As a boy Gyp had taken his advice. Maybe he would listen
now. He moved very quietly to the platform. The conductor was
working with the car door.

Rud asked, "What yuh doin', Gyp?"

Gyp dropped his lantern, turned very slowly.

"Oh, it's you? Well, there was a horse down in this car. I was
tryin' to get it up."

The door was closed and apparently sealed. Rud looked into
the car, and then at Gyp.

"Did the black fillies," he asked, "crawl out through a
crack?"

"The black fillies? Oh!" Gyp grinned sheepishly. "No, the
Southwestern decided I needed them horses, Rud."

"Another payment on the old right-of-way account, eh?"

"Sure!"

Gyp looked at his watch. Rud looked at Gyp.

"I've thought ever since I came back this was what you were
up to," he reproved.

"Well, what of it?"

"You're headed for trouble, Gyp. One of these nights a bull
will sneak on you as I did now."

"I'm a careful nan, Rud. I always take care there's no bull on
my train before I start collectin'."

"There's no thief so slick but that there's a law slick enough
to catch him."

Gyp sneered. "Why don't you report me?"

"You'd be surprised if I did."

"You'd be surprised, if you did. Yes, you would. Listen, Rud. We might as well come clean with each other. I had this thing all figgered out before I ever started it on a big scale. See these?" he pointed to his lodge emblems.

"Yes. I recognize some of them."

"I knew when I started this trail that if I got caught before I got rich, I would need strong arms to defend me. That's why I joined everything in sight, and became a brother to every man of influence in this city."

He did not wait for a reply, but returned to the engine, and when No. 5 had cleared, pulled toward Rover.

IV

A Car for New Orleans

LEAVES came off the calendar. Gyp wisecracked. Rud did not laugh. Often he saw Travis driving away from Jim Weatherby's as he walked down. Sneering, superior, cynical, Gyp saw that he did, and Rud came to resent him bitterly.

In March he told Molly some things she ought to know. Molly gave him back his diamond.

"I'll soon be wearing another, anyway," she said sweetly.

Rud was calm. He said, "All right, Molly, if you'd rather have—a—Gyp than me, take him."

"Of course, we can still be friends," she reminded him.

"Sure. Gyp and I used to be very good friends."

"Why not now?"

Randall did not tell her what Gyp was. Her father had told her, and she had refused to believe it.

He wrote Rawlins, Pocatello, Fort Smith, Las Vegas, Tucson. Early in April, he had a letter from a friend in Pocatello. He might get on firing there around pay day, with prospects of a throttle in the fall.

He debated whether or not to go. While he was debating the spring rains set in. On the morning of the 8th he brought up a banana train. Creeks and rivers were out of their banks. Black water was spilling under every bridge and trestle. Passing Big Breakdown, he noticed that both it and China Pig hole were full halfway to their rims with black water, on which floated froth and leaves and sticks.

There was a wedding announcement on the table for him when he went to his boarding house. He knew what it was before he opened it. With a strange emptiness in his heart, he went up to his room. He packed his grip, took everything out of the dresser drawers, removed Molly's picture from the frame, and put the picture in the bottom of his stationery box. When he had finished, he went to the office to tell Superintendent Bain he was resigning.

White-haired Superintendent Bain belonged to every order, wore every lodge emblem Gyp Travis did—and some Gyp had not heard of. Lodge was his religion.

For a year the railroad law had been telling him Gyp was their arch thief. "A regular box car kleptomaniac." Bain simply ref used to believe it. No man who had taken the vows Gyp had taken could be other than a good citizen. He pointed to Gyp's railroad record, "A sheet without a splotch," to his generosity; he defied the law to prove anything.

The law could prove nothing, for in those days catching and convicting a box car robber was as difficult as convicting a boot-legger under prohibition. Evidence was elusive. Bain refused to discharge him on flimsy pretext, and Gyp worked on.

Losses mounted. Merchandise cars were gutted. In the spring the general office sent new bulls to Wellfield. They worked method-ically. Through the bank they checked on Travis Bros. business. Travis Bros. showed profits out of all proportion to their volume.

The firm bought little and sold much.

THESE new agents rode Gyp's freight trains. Other bulls had done that. They accomplished nothing. On those short trains, against the glow of the firebox, keen eyes looking for them would spot them before they had ridden a mile. And when they rode, nothing happened.

They set watchmen in Travis Hollow; Travis Bros. had good dogs. They planted marked merchandise; Gyp scented marked merchandise as a wise wolf scents poisoned meat. The Southwestern paid; Gyp collected and laughed at them.

The day when Rud went to the office, Bain was busy. The clerk showed him a chair and went to lunch. Behind the frosted door were voices. Rud was no eavesdropper, but he could not help hearing

"I tell you it's him. I know it. We're goin' to catch him in the act. We're goin' to do it quick, too, if we can get a little co-operation from the freight house bunch, from the yard force, and from your office."

"You may be assured of all possible co-operation from this office, and from the service under it, Mr. Jenkins." Superintendent Bain was sincere. "Every honest man on this division will lend his aid in bringing a thief to justice, no matter who he is."

Rud left. He did not try to see Bain again that day. He let his card stay on the board. What did a few days more or less matter?

Wellfield was the hub for six divergent railway lines. Every night trains brought cars of mixed freight which yard crews spotted on the four tracks behind the transfer platform. Sometimes there were a dozen cars to the track, their doors all neatly lined for reloading.

Many cars contained freight for different destinations. A car from Chicago might carry consignments for Memphis, New

Orleans, Arkansas or Texas points. It was the job of the freight house gang to sort this freight, reload it, and head it toward its destination.

Every morning a force of workmen gathered on the platform. They broke the seals, opened the doors. The "breaker-out" entered the car, removed its contents piece by piece, calling to his "checker" the nature and destination of each parcel. The "checker" marked it off the bill of lading. It was loaded on a hand truck, which was given a card, indicating to what runway and what car it was going.

Truckers trundled these hand cars to their alley. The "stever" packed the load into the car and his "checker" marked against it. All day the process continued. At night cars were sealed, billed, and dragged out by switch engines to be made into trains and again sent on their way.

THAT afternoon a New Orleans car was spotted at the east end of the platform, just behind the freight house. A new "stever" was working it. He stowed truckload after truckload of parcels carefully. Certain cases he put at what would be the rear end as the car went southward. Others he put toward the left side. He did not load it evenly. When he had finished, the forward end was empty except for a dozen cases of dry goods and two crated bathtubs. He did not display any surprise over the fact that these bathtubs were light — "damned light for bathtubs," as the trucker said when he brought the last one.

The sealer came with his sealing iron, he threaded the seal wire through the car fastener and through the seal hole and pressed it with his sealing iron, stamping upon one side his station number.

A switch crew came. The foreman had orders to let No. 1 track ride for awhile. He wondered why. He switched the other three tracks, leaving the one with the New Orleans car, and took a transfer to the freight yards.

After he had gone, the new "stever" and two other men came to the New Orleans car. They all went inside. Only one of them came out. He resealed the car. An hour later the switch crew came back, coupled up, took another transfer to the freight yards, and shunted the New Orleans car into Track 1, where No. 55 was making up.

Hi Wells was regular conductor on No. 55. The *new* caller could not find him that night, though Hi declared next day he was at home in bed. Neither could the *new* caller find Jinks Wilson, who was first out on the conductor's extra board. He soon found Gyp Travis and called him for the merchandise. Gyp did not think much about it, because he had often tipped callers four bits in the morning, and thus had been easy to find when a good run was coming up at night.

He was called for 9.05. He went to the yards, checked his train, and signed his orders. The sky was again overcast. Dull, ominous thunder, like the rumble of wheels on the ridge in the Breakdowns, sounded in the heavens. Gyp separated his orders and strode toward the engine with them.

Rans Gaston was regular engineer. He was an old man. When he started down the steps to meet Gyp, he hung his heel on a splinter in the deck, pitched out of the gangway, and broke an arm. Gyp told the dispatcher, who told the roundhouse. The roundhouse sent for an engineer and found Rud Randall, who took the call.

Gyp was waiting when Rud came to the engine. He was gay tonight, because only yesterday his wedding announcements had been mailed.

"How's tricks?" he kidded when he handed Rud the flimsies.

"O.K., I reckon."

"Comin' to the weddin'?"

Rud held out his hand. "Congratulations, Gyp!" he said softly.

Gyp was taken off guard. He laid an impulsive hand on Rud's arm,

"I'm sorry, old-timer," he said. "Really, I am." For the moment he was, too.

Rud said, "That's all right, Gyp. Faint heart—you know—"

"Yes, I know!" Gyp stammered a bit. Maybe he remembered.

Rud remembered, too. He remembered a lot of things quite suddenly. He remembered the night he and Gyp had driven the woods road, remembered the night he had seen Gyp and Ed take a span of horses from a car at Travis Hollow, remembered a few words he had heard through the office wall that morning. He also remembered years ago, when Gyp had come for him in the Bluff Hole.

He cleared his throat, looked up from reading the orders. Gyp was watching the lightning which shimmered over the western hills. Rud folded the orders and put them in his overalls.

"Gyp, if you'll take a tip from a friend, you'll quit collectin', quit it now, and quit it cold."

"Been havin' more nightmares?"

"I'm not sayin' what I've been havin', and I've not talked to anybody. But if you've got as much sense as you think you have, you'll figure you've collected in full from the Southwestern, mark the account paid, wipe the glue off your fingers and keep it off."

"Thanks for the tip, Rud. I'm goin' to quit when I get married."

"You'd better quit before you get married."

"When do we leave town?"

"When you're ready."

"Let's go!"

Gyp flourished his lantern. A light flashed on the rear, another cavorted from the middle of the train.

V

Collected in Full

GYP settled to his office work immediately on leaving Wellfield. Despite the jerk and sway of the caboose, he wrote a neat hand. He made a wheel report, a switch list, and checked his waybills.

That was one job Gyp always did perfectly. He went through the containers. He looked disappointed until he came to the bills on a Pennsylvania car for New Orleans. He chuckled, and a wide grin cracked his face. It was the only car of usable merchandise in the train, but what a car!

There were shoes from Lynn, Mass.; cases of piece goods from Kansas City; men's suits from St. Louis; and best of all, nine cases of "dry goods" from a silk factory in Paterson, N.J., to a jobbing house in New Orleans.

Gyp did not pause to wonder what that silk was doing west of the Mississippi. He made a hasty mental calculation. The silk would be worth up in the thousands.

"Ye gods!" he muttered. "The Southwestern must know I'm goin' to be married."

When No. 55 left Wellfield, Gyp figured they would let No. 5 by at Ludwig. As he ran into Ludwig Rud began calling for a signal. Bennie Weimer, the hind man, called, "Red board, Gyp!"

"I'll get it, Bennie," Gyp called back.

He took his lantern to the rear platform and picked up the order. It said No. 55 would run 40 minutes late from Wellfield to Ludwig, 30 minutes late from Ludwig to Rover, and 20 minutes late from Rover to Sayer.

Gyp handed Bennie the sheet, who read the order and hooked it. Gyp went back to finish his reports. When they were done he joined Bennie in the cupola, where the latter was smoking a foul pipe.

When they stopped for water at Pine Ridge Bennie went out to look over his train. Gyp took a light, stout rope ladder from his grip. He hesitated, looked at his train book. He would not need this rope ladder tonight, because the New Orleans car had end doors. He replaced the ladder in his grip and followed Bennie toward the engine.

He stopped at the Pennsylvania box car, removed the seal, unfastened the catch, and hooked the broken seal back into it. Then he went to the engine. Rud was oiling around. Neither engineer nor conductor said where they would go for the Express.

They left Pine Ridge, thundered through Lathrop, and whistled for Glennwood. Rud did not whistle through. Gyp came out of his seat, fumbling at the window.

"Why, that mudheel don't aim to head in here, I hope?" he rasped.

"He'd better. He ain't got time to go to Rover."

"He's got time to go to Travis Hollow."

"Who wants to head in down in that hole? You don't make any time. You'd be better off to stay here an' let the express by."

But Gyp was not listening. He snatched his lantern off the hook and leaped out on top of the train, swinging a highball.

Rud answered his signal. The slack went out of the train. Gyp peered ahead. The order signal was out for them. He tuned toward the caboose, then changed his mind.

"Bennie'll get it," he muttered.

He was on the second car then. The engine had passed the station. Rud whistled a long, tapered highball. Gyp went to the New Orleans car and set his lantern on the running board. He always did this because brakemen, seeing it there, would think he was out on top because he was a good railroader.

AS calmly as if he were unlocking his caboose, Gyp removed the seal from the fastener, dropped it into a jumper pocket with a track torpedo, and opened the end door. Very calmly and very casually, he removed a dark lantern from his juniper pocket. He had told the boys that was for emergency.

He played it carefully over the interior of the car to make sure no one was in it. Certain he was unobserved, he climbed through the door and eased himself down on the stack of boxes.

The train rolled through Glennwood, climbed the sag beyond, and roared toward the Breakdowns. Gyp referred to a little black book. The cases he wanted were marked "Connati & Co., New Orleans, La." He hoped they were not in the rear end, because the rear end was packed full. He went to the front. He found two crated bathtubs, moved one of them a trifle.

"Some helluva tub," he muttered. "Must be made of lead."

He did not examine them closely. He was looking for silk, and he found it stacked against the left side of the car.

"Thanks, Southwestern!" he muttered. "Some railroads would have stacked this stuff in the back end and piled ten tons on top of it."

He chuckled. He began moving the few cases between the silk and the door. making a lane to move it through. The train roared on. Rud was sure wheeling them.

"Ornery devil must be goin' somewhere for the varnish. Well, let him. I'll unload these boxes on the lam. Ed always checks the right-of-way after a merchandise train runs, just to see if anything's fell off." He laughed.

In the forward end of the car a crated bathtub rose up six inches and settled slowly, but Gyp didn't see it. He was moving cases of silk. A moment later, the other bathtub gave forth a gentle tearing sound. Gyp didn't hear it, because the train was roaring toward the Breakdowns. A moment later a pair of eyes peered through a crack and the crack grew into a porthole.

The storm was overhauling the merchandise train. The box car swayed and lunged. Wheels sang a dull song, deadened as they raced through a cut.

Two of the five cases were at the door and the door was opened. Gyp was taking his time now, but he would have to move quickly when the train ran through Travis Hollow. He turned back to get the third case. He was whistling. As the pilot wheels struck the ridge north of Big Breakdown, Gyp grinned. He thought, "Poor old pap! If he'd only called on his son instead of the Almighty!"

There his thought stopped. Lightning streaked up the sky. The inside of that car was as bright as noon. Gyp's eyes flashed wide. In the gleam of lightning he saw a bathtub sink to the floor. He saw the barrel of a .45 sticking from a hole in the other. He whirled to the open door. A shot rang out.

RUD had a new Mogul on the merchandise that night. Its drivers were low; its speed was slow. He came down on Glennwood sixteen minutes ahead of the Midnight Express. He reckoned he had not time to go to Rover, because he could get no speed from that low-wheeled engine.

He shut off, intending to head in. He saw Gyp come out of the caboose swinging a highball. He commenced swearing,

"I suppose," he raved, "the dirty crook wants to unload another cargo at Travis Hollow. Well, we'll fool him once. We'll go to Rover."

Then he saw the order board. He chuckled, because he guessed there was more time on No. 5. The fireman picked up the tissue. Rud read it. It said the last order was annulled. No. 5 was now to run one hour and 20 minutes late from Ludwig to Glennwood, and one hour late from Glennwood to Sayer.

Instead of 16 minutes ahead of the Express, he was now almost an hour.

"We'll go to Sayer ahead of 'em!" He exulted.

All the way from Wellfield they had been having headlight trouble. A cracked glass let wind into the lamp and it would not stay lighted. Five times the fireman had been out on the pilot of the engine, relighting that lamp.

Two miles out of Gleenwood it flicked out again. The profane fireman started out. Rud called to him, "Hi, Harry. You twist her tail awhile, an' I'll go light it."

The fireman slipped into Rud's seat. Rud took a piece of waste, went through the front window, followed the running board, and stood on a four-by-six step on the end of the boiler.

Before lighting the lamp, he poked a piece of waste into the crack, He finished just as they reached the ridge north of Big Breakdown. When they rounded the curve and started over the ridge, he turned to peer ahead. Ever since he had been here, some impulse from within had made him always look ahead when he approached this ridge. Black water was far up toward the rim of Big Breakdown.

The wheels struck the ridge. The hollow echo started as it always did when trains ran over it. For a fraction of a second the sound continued. Then it ceased—ceased as suddenly as it had begun.

The earth shook like a jelly roll. The engine tilted right, heeled left, and kept going. Rud had never been in a wreck, but he knew he was turning over. He thought it had left the track and headed for China Pighole. He turned loose and jumped toward Big Breakdown.

He knew distinctly when he was in the air. He knew he was going to get hurt. He realized vaguely when he hit the earth. Then he was in water up to his waist. The water revived him. There was a ringing in his ears. His mind was playing strange tricks on him. He was back in the old Bluff hole, with the cramps. He was going down and the water was closing over him. He tried to get out, fought for freedom, settled lower into the water and called, "Gyp! Oh, Gyp?"

He thought there was an answering shout.

INCH by inch the water crept up his sides. No help came. He remembered now that he was not in the old swimming hole. He had been on an engine and the engine had left the track. Groping about him, he found he was lying on his back on a wall of steeply sloping earth, and water was rising.

Lightning came. He turned his head and saw he was in a pit.

Rud Jumped as the Engine Left the Track

Above him towered jagged walls. He started up in terror, knowing what had happened. His train had not merely wrecked. That ridge had caved in. The thing his father and Jed Travis had foreseen, had prayed for and hoped for, had finally come. Flood and freshet had undermined the structure, weakened roof supports, and let the ridge fall and take his train to destruction.

He tried to get up, but his right leg was dead. His effort dragged

him lower because the steeply sloping pile of debris was settling. Water was now almost to his neck.

The light came again. He was rational now. He glanced keenly about. The entire backbone had caved in. Where the ridge had stood with a railroad running over it, was now only a great jagged pit. He was lying on the debris at the eastern end of it. A sheer limestone wall was rising above him.

The center of the pit was filled with the wreckage of a Mogul, fifteen freight cars and a freight caboose. Some of the cars were on their sides; others were smashed to pieces. One was up-ended, leaning against the west wall. Wrapped around it, hanging from the top of the bluff, was a patchwork of twisted steel rails.

All this he saw, and more. To right and left toward old sink-holes, were now ridges of earth. Etched against the lightning, they appeared as two gigantic "U's," one on each side of the pit, with saplings leaning over, some of them buried beneath the water which was spilling rapidly from the Big Breakdown.

He thought he was doomed. That water would rise about his neck, his chin, his mouth, his nostrils. He turned his eyes in the third flash to his immediate surroundings. Twenty feet away along the edge of the pit was a gnarled hickory sapling.

Distinctly he remembered it. He and Gyp had caught a possum out of it that night nine years ago when Travis Hollow bridge had burned.

"Gyp! Oh, Gyp!" he called.

He thought he heard a low spoken answer. A moment later a hoarse voice croaked: "Where are you?"

THE lightning came. He could see a man creeping along the ridge next the Breakdown. it was Gyp Travis, He was coming slowly toward him, like a body seeking its soul, bending almost double, clutching at his side. Gyp came to the fallen hickory, looked down upon him,

The hickory reached forty feet into the pit. Its top lapped over the wreckage, now fast sinking from sight. Gyp crawled out on its trunk. Like one in a trance, he reached a scantling, drew it dazedly toward him, dropped it into the water at Rud's head. Rud caught it and worked it to the pit wall. It sank into the water and held.

Gyp shoved down another scantling, and still another, until there was a crude platform, part under water, part above, reaching from the sloping debris to the wreckage.

Rud laid hold the platform and tried to climb upon it. He could not lift himself. Gyp came fumbling down to the platform. He gave Rud a hand, pulled. Rud screamed. That foot had now come alive. He thought Gyp was tearing him to pieces, but he did not seem to hear.

Rud swooned, and when he came to, he and Gyp were on the ridge above Big Breakdown. Rud sat up and felt of his foot. The ankle was smashed; the foot horribly twisted. He almost fainted. Gyp bent low over him and said thickly, "Looks like—the old man got his prayer answered at last."

Rud nodded. Gyp coughed several times and sat down.

"I reckon I'm done for, old-timer."

"Done for!" Rud had not been aware that Gyp was seriously hurt. He peered through the darkness. Another flash of light. Gyp's face was ghastly, and pink froth was on his lips. "What—what's the matter?"

Rud forgot his own injuries now. He tried to get up. Gyp spoke huskily. The railroader was talking.

"Look out for No. 5."

Rud had forgotten No. 5. He remembered that he had got an order at Glennwood, and that the Express had been an hour away. He wondered why Gyp had not got that order. Then he recalled the conductor had been on top of the train.

Gyp was squatted on his haunches. His head was coming lower. Rud crawled to him, took him by the shoulder.

"What's the matter? Where are you hurt?"

"I'm shot." Gyp straightened his shoulders a trifle and leaned toward Rud. His voice was like the cough of a foaming engine.

"You was right. Right about—what you told me."

Rud held Gyp's weakening head and listened.

"I was collectin'—again … Collectin' the last payment off the Southwestern. There was two bulls sealed in a car. One of 'em got me!"

Rud said nothing. He remembered the two fathers, teaching their sons to hate, and cry for vengeance. Now vengeance had come.

Gyp's breath grew louder, shorter. His cough came more frequently. He muttered thickly, "flag five—don't forget."

He had quit breathing when Rud fumbled in the soaked jumper for the torpedo which he knew Gyp always carried. Rud had found it and also a broken car seal. He slipped the torpedo in his own pocket and threw the seal far out into the sink-hole.

The storm struck. Wind whipped rain into his face, and into that other face. The stream of water from Big Breakdown to the new "vengeance" hole was growing larger, and more earth was caving in.

Rud crawled painfully across the stream. Every inch was agony. He crawled up the steep embankment to the track, and down the track toward Glennwood.

Through that half-mile, dragging a broken ankle, he crawled a thousand years—or so it seemed.

In Rud's glimmering consciousness, ghost lights danced on before. He scarcely knew when Big Jim Weatherby answered his signal.

He did not know when he was carried into the coach and placed on some cushions. He did know when Molly came to see him. She asked him how Gyp had gone. He patted her hand and told her part of it. He did not tell her everything. For the ridge where he had left Gyp lying had caved away, burying a body with its last tell-tale mark of vengeance.

Who's Who in the Crew

by Stookie Allen

AMERICA'S FOREMOST RAILROAD FICTION WRITER WAS BORN AT NORWOOD, MO., JUNE 1, 1886. AT AGE OF 4 HE TOOK HIS FIRST TRAIN RIDE TO ATTEND THE WEDDING OF HIS FUTURE MOTHER-IN-LAW.

AFTER WORKING AS A GANDY DANCER ON THE "KATY," AND TEACHING SCHOOL, HE GOT A JOB BREAKING FREIGHT ON THE MO.P. THROUGH THE EFFORTS OF HIS BROTHER, CONDUCTOR BILL DELLINGER. LATER, HE AND BILL WENT INTO FRISCO TRAIN SERVICE. BIGGEST THRILL WAS RIDING ATOP A PASSENGER COACH ON THE FRISCO "CANNON BALL" IN 1908. ONCE IN 1920, A TRAIN CREW CONTAINED 4 DELLINGERS: BILL, E.S., AND 2 OF BILL'S SONS.

E.S. DELLINGER

E.S. QUIT THE ROAD, GRADUATED FROM NEW MEXICO NORMAL UNIV. IN 1923, AND SERVED AS SUPT. OF PUBLIC SCHOOLS AT SPRINGER, N.M. (1925-33), MEANWHILE WRITING FOR VARIOUS MAGAZINES. MOST OF HIS STORIES ARE NOVELETTES. 50 OF THEM APPEARED IN **RAILROAD MAN'S** AND **RAILROAD STORIES**, BEGINNING WITH "REDEMPTION FOR SLIM" (DEC 1929). DELLINGER IS MARRIED, HAS A DAUGHTER ROSEMARY AND A SON DALE, AND LIVES IN ALBUQUERQUE, N.M. HIS BEST KNOWN CHARACTERS ARE:

BRICK DONLEY

KING LAWSON

REDHOT FROST

RUD RANDALL

The Lure of
Railroad Stories

Railroad Stories Magazine (as it is more commonly known) debuted in 1906 as *Railroad Man's Magazine*, published by the Frank A. Munsey Company. The publication merged with *Argosy* in 1919 magazine, but the series was revived a decade later.

Nonfiction articles pertained to the history and operation of various railroads across the world (primarily in the United States of America). Authors often penned personal essays about their experiences and observations of the rails.

Fiction was another popular feature. Short stories and novels featured a variety of recurring characters and their adventures. Sometimes it became difficult to tell where fiction and fact ended — several of the regular authors were former (and current) railroad employees, and they knew the minutia of railroad procedures and operations.

In 1943, the Frank A. Munsey Company sold *Railroad Stories* to Popular Publications, Inc., which also acquired *Argosy* magazine. As the U.S.A. became embroiled in World War II, fiction gradually decreased to one story per issue. New stories alternated with reprints throughout the 1960s until 1979, when *Railroad Magazine* (now owned by Carsten Publishing) ceased publication in 1979.

More great titles from Bold Venture Press ...

Once a Pulp Man: The Secret Life of Judson P. Philip as Hugh Pentecost
by Audrey Parente

Judson P. Philips, author of *Cancelled in Red*, had two lucrative writing careers. He filled pages in magazines like *Argosy* under his own name, and wrote for slick magazines and paperbacks as Hugh Pentecost. *Once a Pulp Man* unveils the author whose personal life was as complicated as any mystery plot.

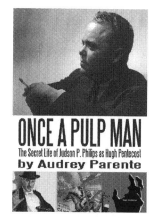

The Galaxy Queen *by John R. Rose*

Ruben Hall never planned to be a star-spanning hero! He was an ordinary teenager — until he was given the opportunity to join the elite Space Rangers corps! Accompanied by his girlfriend and plucky uncle, Ruben Hall quickly becomes an interstellar legend! But before he can say "Warp Speed," he's an intergalactic outlaw with a price on his head!

Alias the Kansas Kid
by John R. Rose

Dan Robbins wasn't looking for trouble, but trouble found him. He sought to carve out a life in the Kansas rangeland's Red Hills, rejecting his father's outlaw methods. Too bad he demonstrated the same proficiency with a gun. Folks wouldn't leave well enough alone — they *just had to* challenge the Kansas Kid.

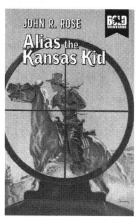

www.boldventurepress.com

Continuing series from Bold Venture Press ...

Zorro: The Complete Pulp Adventures
Six volumes by Johnston McCulley
In the early 1800s, California was still under Spanish rule. Some of the military commanders plundered and won riches at the expense of the peace-loving settlers. Against these agents of injustice, the settlers were powerless, until one man arose whose courage inspired Californians and gave them the spirit to resist tyranny. *That man was Zorro!*

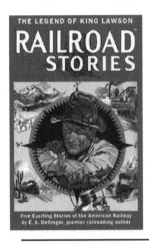

Railroad Stories
Adventure on the American railways!
All aboard for romance, danger, and plain old American hard work! Classic pulp fiction tales of the railways! For decades, readers were entertained each month with *Railroad Stories Magazine* and it's blend of factual articles and fiction yarns. This is wholesome he-man fiction for railroad fans, written by authors who knew trains first-hand!

Pulp Adventures
Every issue is a voyage across the landscape of pulp fiction — mystery, science fiction, horror, romance, western, and more! from lush jungles to sun-baked deserts, lawless wild west towns to utopian cities of the future! Don your pith helmets and fedoras and embark on great reading!

www.boldventurepress.com

Made in the USA
Middletown, DE
28 October 2020